Put ~~~~~ in it,
Percy!

Percy was a treasure. He cleaned and polished and scrubbed and washed and gardened and ironed. Sometimes he went out on mysterious errands and came back with carrots and onions and lettuce and grapes and other things to eat. "Amazing," said Mr Fooby-Lartil. "How does he do it?"

"Don't ask," said Mrs Fooby-Lartil.

And things would have gone on very happily if only Mr Fooby-Lartil had never decided to invent his New-All-Purpose-Marvellous-Body-Safe-Stick-Anything-Anywhere-Anytime-Glue.

Scholastic Children's Books,
Commonwealth House,
1-19 New Oxford Street,
London WC1A 1NU, UK
A division of Scholastic Ltd
London ~ New York ~ Toronto ~ Sydney ~ Auckland

First published in the UK by Scholastic Ltd, 1994
This edition, 1997

ISBN 0 590 19916 1

Typeset by Contour Typesetters, Southall, London
Printed by Cox and Wyman Ltd, Reading, Berkshire

10 9 8 7 6 5 4 3 2 1

HIPPO **FUNNY**

Put a sock in it, Percy!

Judy Corbalis

illustrated by David Parkins

Hippo

For Tom

Chapter 1

"Look out!" yelled Mr Fooby-Lartil from the garden. A tongue of flame shot through the shed roof. Up in her attic inventing room, Mrs Fooby-Lartil ducked as a small piece of metal zinged in at the window, past her ear and out through the roof.

KEEP OUT

She leaned over the sill.

"It's all right," called Mr Fooby-Lartil. "Just my Totally-Troublefree-Time-Tested-Teamaker. It's exploded again."

Mrs Fooby-Lartil sighed. "I don't see why you don't let me help you with it," she said. "That's the fifth time it's blown up."

Black streaks covered Mr Fooby-Lartil's face. "But this time I've cracked it!" he shouted. "It was the whistling valve."

"It's made another hole in the roof," said Mrs Fooby-Lartil.

"Don't worry," said Mr Fooby-Lartil. "I'll fill that up with glue." He looked at the sky. "Lucky it's not raining."

"It's lunch-time," said Mrs Fooby-Lartil, leaning further out of the window. "Are you coming in now?"

"Right away!" cried Mr Fooby-Lartil, rubbing at his face and smearing soot all over his cheeks. "I'll just put back the fire extinguisher and wash up a bit. Good news about the Teamaker, isn't it?"

Mrs Fooby-Lartil put away her spanner and

went downstairs.

"What's for lunch?" said Mr Fooby-Lartil. "I'm starving."

"I don't know," said Mrs Fooby-Lartil. "You're on cooking today."

"No, you do Tuesday," said Mr Fooby-Lartil. "It's my turn on Wednesday."

"Today *is* Wednesday," said Mrs Fooby-Lartil.

"Really," said Mr Fooby-Lartil. "What on earth happened to Tuesday?"

"It just went," said his wife. "Yesterday. What's for lunch?"

Mr Fooby-Lartil looked in the larder. "Nothing," he said mournfully.

"What about the bacon rind and the scraps of cheese?"

"I think the mice have had them," said Mr Fooby-Lartil.

"Those mice are getting altogether too big for their boots," said his wife.

"Maybe we should get a trap," said Mr Fooby-Lartil.

Mrs Fooby-Lartil stared at him in horror.

"They can't help being mice," she said. "It's not their fault they take our food. I expect they're hungry too."

"They're better fed than we are right now," said her husband. "I'd even say yes if the Grimbotts offered us some apples."

"Well, you know they won't," said Mrs Fooby-Lartil. "Mean pigs."

"Their apples look really tasty," said Mr Fooby-Lartil. "And there's nothing I can't do with an apple. D'you remember last year when we had all those free ones from the farmer? Apple cake, apple sauce, apple fritters, apple pudding, apple tart, apple turnovers, apple juice, apple tea, apple pie, stewed apple, baked apple, boiled apple, apple pancakes, apple porridge, apple soup . . ."

"I remember," said Mrs Fooby-Lartil, "and they were all delicious, of course. But . . . apples for every single meal . . ."

Mr Fooby-Lartil looked hurt. "Better than no food at all," he said, peering into the empty larder again. "Maybe I could find some blackberries. There were lots last week on the road out of town. I could make blackberry and apple pie without the apple."

Mrs Fooby-Lartil winced. "Good idea," she said bravely. "But you'll have to go on your own. I need to finish off my Self-Making Bed."

"Right," said Mr Fooby-Lartil. He took off his double-strength inventing specs, put on his ordinary pair, left his pipe on the table and picked up the gramophone horn from the shelf. "This should be big enough," he said and swung off into the lane.

Mrs Fooby-Lartil's stomach was rumbling loudly. She searched in the larder and found three raisins and a coffee bean. "Things are getting a bit desperate," she said to herself as she climbed back up to her inventing room in the attic.

There was a noise below in the kitchen. She ran downstairs just in time to see three fat mice scurrying into the larder. "Not *again*," said Mrs Fooby-Lartil. She slipped out to the shed and brought back the Fooby-Lartil-Sure-to-Succeed-Knock-On-Knock-Down-Household-Mouse-Terrifier, carefully set it up outside the

larder door and activated it. The mice shot out of the larder at once.

"Oh dear," said Mrs Fooby-Lartil. "He's right. If this goes on we *will* have to get a mousetrap." And she went back upstairs.

She knelt down beside the Self-Making Bed. She had put a big flat foot on each leg to make moving the bed easier. And there was a hand on each corner so the Bed could make itself when she pulled a switch. "Nearly finished," she said to herself. "And this could be the invention that makes our fortune. After all, everyone sleeps in a bed and everyone hates having to make it in the morning."

"No toenails," she decided, tightening up the feet. "Someone will only have to cut them. And they'd better be clean feet, not smelly." She dropped oil of roses into the slits on top of each foot. A lovely smell drifted around the attic. "Mmm," said Mrs Fooby-Lartil, sniffing.

She pulled the switch. The hands at the bottom began smoothing and tucking the sheet, the hands at the top tucked in the other end and shook and plumped the pillows. Mrs Fooby-Lartil was pleased. "Tomorrow night

we'll sleep in it," she thought. She leaned out of
the window to see if there was any sign of Mr
Fooby-Lartil.

There he was, racing along the road clutching the gramophone horn. And he'd taken off
his shirt. Mrs Fooby-Lartil waved. "Did you
get any blackberries?" she called but Mr
Fooby-Lartil was too far away to hear. He
certainly had something in the horn and he
seemed very agitated. It couldn't be black-

berries: he was running too fast. "He's found something special," thought Mrs Fooby-Lartil and her spirits rose. Maybe it was mushrooms, or a fish, or even a chicken. She ran downstairs, turned on the stove, then hurried out to meet him.

"What is it?" she cried but he was too short of breath to answer. Whatever was inside the horn was wrapped up in his shirt. It must be a fish: the shirt was all wet.

"I've turned on the stove," she said. "Come and show me what you've got."

Chapter 2

Mr Fooby-Lartil put the horn on the table and took a deep breath. "Found it," he puffed. "In the pond."

It *was* a fish. Mrs Fooby-Lartil was delighted. Blackberries were better than nothing, of course, but they weren't really very filling. Mr Fooby-Lartil knelt by the stove. "Get a towel," he said. "Quick. And some newspaper."

"A towel?" she said, puzzled.

"Hurry," he said, lifting the horn down beside him and unwrapping the shirt. Mrs Fooby-Lartil handed him the towel.

"Here," she said. "I . . ."

She stopped in surprise. Inside the towel was a soaking wet, half-drowned, very ugly cat with half an ear missing, crooked whiskers and a kink in its tail. "We can't eat that," she said.

The cat gave a terrified water-logged gurgle.

"Eat him?" said Mr Fooby-Lartil. "Who said anything about eating him?"

"But what's he doing here?" said Mrs Fooby-Lartil.

"I found him," said Mr Fooby-Lartil. "In the duck-pond."

"No wonder your trousers are all wet," said Mrs Fooby-Lartil. "I thought you'd been fishing."

Mr Fooby-Lartil sneezed.

"I'll dry him," said Mrs Fooby-Lartil, taking the towel. "You go and have a hot bath."

Mr Fooby-Lartil picked up the intercom and spoke to the bath control panel. "Bath," he said. "Three-quarters full. Medium hot. No bubbles. Right away. Thank you."

Mrs Fooby-Lartil was drying the cat. "Poor thing," she said. "He's nearly drowned."

"He would have been in two more minutes," said Mr Fooby-Lartil. "I'd just gone past the duckpond when there was a huge splash. I swung round and caught sight of someone slipping into the bushes and then I saw big ripples in the pond. I thought someone had thrown a stone."

"And then?" said Mrs Fooby-Lartil.

"I heard a faint yowl," said Mr Fooby-

Lartil, "and I saw a long furry paw sinking into the water. They'd tied him in a sack but he'd managed to get one leg free."

Mrs Fooby-Lartil was indignant. "How wicked," she said. "What happened then?"

"I plunged in straight away," said Mr Fooby-Lartil, "but I had to feel round for the sack and by the time I got him onto the bank, he was nearly dead. So I wrapped him in my shirt, put him in the horn and raced home."

Mrs Fooby-Lartil went to the larder and took out the very last of the milk. She poured it into a saucer, added a bit of warm water and put it down in front of the cat. He was drying out nicely. "Poor thing," she said.

"I expect he'd better have the tin of sardines," said Mr Fooby-Lartil. "It's hidden under the mixing bowl. I've been saving it for Christmas. Do you mind?"

"Of course not," said Mrs Fooby-Lartil.

Mr Fooby-Lartil tipped the sardines into a bowl. "I've had an idea," he said. "When it's dark, I'll slip over to the Grimbotts' orchard and gather up a few windfalls. You don't mind baked apples for dinner, do you?"

"Heavens, no," said Mrs Fooby-Lartil. "I love apples. You know that. But mind the Grimbotts don't catch you."

The cat raised his head and began to drink. "He's starving," said Mrs Fooby-Lartil.

"Your bath is ready!" boomed the intercom.

Mr Fooby-Lartil patted the cat who had started on the sardines. "Back in a minute," he said.

"We can't keep him, though," said Mrs Fooby-Lartil. "We can't even afford to keep ourselves. We can't possibly keep a cat."

"Tomorrow I'll go and find him a new home," said Mr Fooby-Lartil.

"Or you could take him to the Cats' Home," said Mrs Fooby-Lartil.

The cat gave a pitiful yowl.

"I'll go and have my bath now," said Mr Fooby-Lartil hastily. "Then I'll pinch those apples."

After supper, they put the cat on a cushion in front of the stove. "He's looking much better," said Mr Fooby-Lartil. "But we really can't keep him."

"No question about that," said Mrs Fooby-Lartil. She bent down and stroked him. "Sleep well, Puss," she said. "See you in the morning."

Next morning when the Fooby-Lartils came downstairs, they found all the dishes had been washed and the kitchen floor had been swept. The cat was standing in Mr Fooby-Lartil's apron, washing the windows. On the table were three dead mice, one by Mr Fooby-Lartil's place, one by Mrs Fooby-Lartil's and another on the cat's saucer.

"Oh dear," said Mrs Fooby-Lartil. "This isn't going to be easy." She sat down. The cat jumped onto her lap and began to purr.

"He wants to stay," said Mr Fooby-Lartil.

"I know," said Mrs Fooby-Lartil. "But we'd never manage to feed him." She made them both a cup of tea. "And it's not just the food," she said. "It's the milk as well."

The cat leapt onto Mr Fooby-Lartil's knee, blew on his tea and took a great slurp. "He

doesn't mind drinking tea without milk," said Mr Fooby-Lartil helplessly.

"Sorry, Puss," said Mrs Fooby-Lartil, "but I'm sure you'll like it at the Cats' Home. We'll take you after lunch."

By lunchtime, the cat had cleaned the windows, polished the table and done the washing. "He's wonderfully good at housework," said Mr Fooby-Lartil. "The place has never been so clean."

"You can see out of the windows again," said Mrs Fooby-Lartil. "And I've spent all morning inventing. I haven't had to think about housework once."

"Me too," said Mr Fooby-Lartil. "I suppose we could keep him for a while, anyway. He can catch mice for food."

"Let's try it," said Mrs Fooby-Lartil. "We'll call him Percy, after my uncle." Percy rubbed up against their legs, purring gratefully.

He was a treasure. He cleaned and polished and scrubbed and washed and gardened and ironed. Sometimes he went out on mysterious errands and came back with carrots and onions and lettuce and grapes and other things to eat. "Amazing," said Mr Fooby-Lartil. "How does he do it?"

"Don't ask," said Mrs Fooby-Lartil.

And things would have gone on very happily if only Mr Fooby-Lartil had never decided to invent his New-All-Purpose-Marvellous-Body-Safe-Stick-Anything-Anywhere-Anytime-Glue.

Chapter 3

Mr Fooby-Lartil was very proud of his glue invention. "With ordinary glue," he explained to Mrs Fooby-Lartil, "you don't get ever-lasting stickiness."

"You do with super glue," said Mrs Fooby-Lartil.

"But it sticks your fingers together. And your eyelids, if you don't use it properly," said Mr Fooby-Lartil. "My glue's perfectly safe. *And* it lasts for ever."

"What's in it?" asked Mrs Fooby-Lartil.

"Oh, everything," said Mr Fooby-Lartil. "Horsehair, frog-spawn, jam, chewing-gum, honey, treacle, sweat, fish paste, tar, chestnuts,

ear-wax. . . that sort of thing. I've boiled them
all up and I've added flour and toothpaste to
whiten the mixture. I'll leave it here tonight to
cool, then tomorrow morning, I'll bottle it."

But much later that night they were woken by Percy complaining in the bedroom. "Horrible," he kept muttering. "Just horrible. Vile, terrible stuff."

"You're talking in your sleep again," said Mrs Fooby-Lartil, giving her husband a shove. "Sshh, you're waking me up."

"It isn't me, it's you," he muttered sleepily.

"No, it's you."

"I'll never get rid of that foul taste in my mouth," moaned Percy.

"It's Percy," said Mr Fooby-Lartil, yawning. "He's talking about the glue. He must have taken a lick at it."

"Glue?" said Percy. "Poison, more like."

"Very best glue," murmured Mr Fooby-Lartil, then sat bolt upright. "He's talking!" he shouted. "Percy's talking!"

"Nonsense," said Mrs Fooby-Lartil, still half asleep. "It's you."

"It's not!" cried Mr Fooby-Lartil. "Wake up and see."

And as Mrs Fooby-Lartil opened her eyes, he had a sudden thought.

"The mixture," he exclaimed. "I'll go and put it into a jar right away. We'll be rich. Everyone'll want to have talking animals."

He kissed Mrs Fooby-Lartil. "I always knew we'd invent something really remarkable one of these days and we've done it." He raced down to the kitchen.

"I feel sick," said Percy. "Very sick."

And he threw up on the bedroom carpet.

Mr Fooby-Lartil came back. He looked at Percy crossly.

"You're so greedy," he said. "Fancy eating all of it. I'll have to make another lot tomorrow."

"Just don't ask *me* to taste it for you," said Percy bitterly. "It's nearly killed me and left me a freak. Even the mice were laughing at me. A talking cat. What kind of cat's that? I've a good mind to leave here right away."

Chapter 4

"Look at it this way, Percy," said Mr Fooby-Lartil next morning. "You're special. Unique. There can't be one other talking cat in the world."

Percy looked sulky. "So?" he said.

"So you should be grateful," said Mr Fooby-Lartil.

Percy snorted.

Mrs Fooby-Lartil came clattering downstairs. A plate perched precariously on the Self-Stacking Cupboard fell off and smashed. "Ow! Help!" shrieked Percy. "It might have fallen on my head. I could have been killed."

"It was miles away from you," said Mr

Fooby-Lartil. "Stop being silly."

"That Cupboard's jealous of me," said Percy darkly. "It wants to get me."

"Why on earth would the Cupboard want to get you?" asked Mrs Fooby-Lartil.

"It doesn't like me, that's why," said Percy. "It's uppity. Thinks it's special just because it puts the dishes into itself on its own. You should never have made it self-stacking."

Mr Fooby-Lartil sighed. "It's an ordinary cupboard," he said. "With a few modifications and adjustments. That's all."

"It's not an ordinary cupboard," said Percy. "It's weird. When you weren't looking, it tried to shut my tail in its doors."

As he spoke, the Cupboard's doors sprang open, then shut again.

"See," he said.

"That doesn't prove anything," said Mrs Fooby-Lartil. "It quite often does that."

Percy's complaining was beginning to get on her nerves.

"Look, Percy," she said, making an effort to sound kind, "we're sorry about what's happened, we really are. Would you like us to try to invent something to *stop* you talking?"

Percy looked at her fiercely. "Oh, thank you very much," he said with a bitter laugh. "Wonderful. 'Just try a little bit of this poison, Percy. Test out another foul-tasting mixture for us. You might even sprout wings and find you can fly.' Try out another one of his inventions? Not likely."

"As I recall," said Mr Fooby-Lartil, "nobody asked you to try out anything. You very greedily went and ate it all by yourself after we'd gone to bed. It's your own fault."

Percy looked embarrassed.

"And," Mr Fooby-Lartil went on, "if you're going to go on complaining, perhaps you'd be happier at the Cats' Home."

"I'm not complaining," said Percy. "I just happened to mention it. In passing."

He picked up the dish cloth and ostentatiously began wiping the table.

Mrs Fooby-Lartil thought Mr Fooby-Lartil was being a little harsh. "You might find you really enjoy being able to talk," she said. "I could teach you to read. Would you like that?"

"I can read already, thank you," said Percy stiffly. He rinsed out the dish cloth and started on the counter top. "Filthy, absolutely filthy," he muttered just loud enough to be heard.

Mrs Fooby-Lartil frowned at Mr Fooby-Lartil and shook her head.

"Well, I'll be off out to the shed now," said Mr Fooby-Lartil. He picked up his inventing specs and his pipe. "I only hope I can remember the formula. See you at lunchtime."

Percy boiled the kettle and made some tea for himself and Mrs Fooby-Lartil. He took the cups over to the table and sat down opposite her. "There is one thing I'd like," he said, "but I don't want *him* to hear." He waved a paw in the direction of the shed.

"What's that?" said Mrs Fooby-Lartil.

"The fact is," said Percy, crossing his back paws and taking another draught of tea, "I do have a secret ambition. I've always rather wanted to be an inventor."

"Oh," said Mrs Fooby-Lartil.

"I'm full of good ideas," said Percy. "Slip-on shampoo pads for the paws . . . To save all the licking, you know," he added, noticing Mrs Fooby-Lartil's expression. "And raised saucers so it's easier to get at the food without bending your head right down. And small heating pads to go at the end of the bed and warm it up."

Mrs Fooby-Lartil looked puzzled.

"Some cats," explained Percy, "get to sleep on their owners' beds."

"And some cats," said Mrs Fooby-Lartil, "get to sleep at the Cats' Home."

"Oh, *I* wouldn't want to sleep on anyone's bed," said Percy hastily. "It's just that some cats do."

"Hmm," said Mrs Fooby-Lartil.

"So what do you think?" said Percy. "About the inventions."

"Well," said Mrs Fooby-Lartil, "if I were a cat, I'd be very interested in all of them. And they're certainly original. But most of the time it's people, not cats, who buy inventions. So I don't think they'd be very commercial."

"Commercial?" said Percy. "What's that?"

"It means making money," said Mrs Fooby-Lartil.

"Money," said Percy scornfully. "I'm not talking money. I'm talking ideas. And art."

Mrs Fooby-Lartil just managed to stop herself from saying that Percy was talking far too much. "Money helps buy food," she said instead.

"Oh," said Percy.

"But if you have any good ideas for inventions for people," said Mrs Fooby-Lartil, "maybe we could all work on them together."

"I'm not working with *him*," said Percy. "He wouldn't understand."

"He was the one who brought you home in the first place," said Mrs Fooby-Lartil.

"And nearly . . ." Percy started to say.

"Yes?" said Mrs Fooby-Lartil.

"And saved me from nearly drowning," said Percy quickly. "If I have a good idea for people, I'll let you know right away."

Chapter 5

Mr Fooby-Lartil spent a busy morning in the shed.

"Horsehair, frog-spawn, jam, fish paste," he muttered as he assembled the ingredients. "Now, was it one tablespoonful of jam and two of frog-spawn or two of frog-spawn and one of jam? Or maybe three of jam and one of fish paste. And there was a scraping of ear-wax, I remember. And something else? Tar, maybe? Oh yes, and toothpaste and flour for whitening it." He sat down and scratched his head. What exactly *had* he put in that mixture? He could almost remember but not quite.

By lunchtime, he had made four batches and

not one of them looked the right colour or consistency. "But this afternoon," he told himself, "I'm bound to get it right." He went whistling in for lunch.

"Bad news, I'm afraid," said Mrs Fooby-Lartil. "We've completely run out of everything."

"Where's Percy?" said Mr Fooby-Lartil, looking around.

"Out," said his wife.

"Maybe he'll bring back some potatoes," said Mr Fooby-Lartil. "Or a carrot or something. Remember that bunch of grapes last week? Delicious."

He rubbed his stomach at the thought.

"The fact is," said Mrs Fooby-Lartil, "Percy's being very difficult since he ate your glue. This morning he hardly touched the housework. And when I asked where he was going, he said, 'Out on business, so I won't have time to go hunting for food like any common alley cat.'"

Mr Fooby-Lartil sighed.

"If you ask me," said Mrs Fooby-Lartil, "it was much easier when he just miaowed. I wish you could make an antidote."

"He wouldn't eat it," said Mr Fooby-Lartil. "You know, secretly, I think he's rather proud of being able to talk. I just hope he doesn't get himself into trouble."

"How?" asked his wife.

"Talking animals," said Mr Fooby-Lartil, "would be worth a great deal of money. Look at what people pay for talking parrots. And I've never heard one that talked half as well as Percy."

"So someone might be interested in kidnapping him?" said Mrs Fooby-Lartil.

"It did cross my mind," said Mr Fooby-Lartil. "But I can't think of anyone round here who'd do a mean thing like that."

"Somebody dumped him in the pond," pointed out Mrs Fooby-Lartil.

"True," said her husband.

"With a parrot," said Mrs Fooby-Lartil, "at least you can throw a cloth over its cage at night to keep it quiet. Percy just goes on and on."

"I know," said Mr Fooby-Lartil. "I wish he'd put a sock in it. I've had a bad morning. I've tried four times to make that formula again but I can't get it right."

"Never mind," said Mrs Fooby-Lartil. "Let's think about lunch. Where are we going to get some food?"

"I can't keep pinching the Grimbotts' apples," said Mr Fooby-Lartil.

"It's not really stealing," said Mrs Fooby-Lartil. "They're windfalls. No one else is going to eat them. The Grimbotts pick them up every morning and just throw them away."

"Even so . . ." said Mr Fooby-Lartil.

"Well," said Mrs Fooby-Lartil, "why don't we work out a way of paying back the Grimbotts? There must be something we can do for them in return for the apples."

"But they don't know we've been scrumping them," said Mr Fooby-Lartil. "You're surely not going to tell them?"

"Of course not," said Mrs Fooby-Lartil. "We don't need to mention the apples we've had already. We can just go and ask them if we could swap them some apples for . . . for . . . for . . . a . . . a . . ."

"Yes?" said Mr Fooby-Lartil.

"For a . . . a . . . a . . ."

"A what?"

"A . . . a . . . a . . . scarecrow!" said Mrs Fooby-Lartil triumphantly. "That's it! A scarecrow. That's what they need. To scare the crows off the apples."

"What a wonderful idea," said Mr Fooby-Lartil. "Let's go and see them right away." He paused. "But I thought you said you were sick of eating apples."

"If it's apples or no food at all," said Mrs Fooby-Lartil, "give me apples any day."

Chapter 6

Mr and Mrs Grimbott lived at the other end of the lane. Their cottage was clean and tidy, their grass was neatly mown and, as Mr Grimbott was always saying, everything looked just right. The plants in the garden stood up straight and tall, the paths were swept and the edges of the lawn were clipped back into perfect straight lines. Every morning, Mr Grimbott picked up all the leaves from under the trees in the orchard, collected any apples that had fallen overnight and threw them in the rubbish bin. "They make the place untidy," he explained.

"Quite right," said his wife. "We don't want

it looking like the Fooby-Lartils'."

Mr Grimbott looked shocked. "Certainly not," he agreed.

As Mr and Mrs Fooby-Lartil came in at the Grimbotts' gate, they heard a familiar voice. "Cream and mackerel!" it was saying in disgust. "Cream and mackerel *every day*, the lucky thing."

"Percy!" said Mr Fooby-Lartil sharply. "Come away from that window at once."

Percy dropped down from the kitchen window sill. "The Grimbotts' cat . . ." he began accusingly.

"Percy," said Mr Fooby-Lartil, "put a sock in it."

"Put a sock in what?" said Percy.

"Your mouth," said Mrs Fooby-Lartil. "He's telling you to be quiet."

"Me?" said Percy in hurt tones. "I hardly said a thing."

Mrs Fooby-Lartil gazed at the neat garden, the perfect lawn and the immaculate orchard. "Much too tidy," she shuddered. Mr Fooby-

Lartil nodded as he struck the knocker.

Mr Grimbott looked surprised to see the Fooby-Lartils and Percy on his doorstep. "What do you want?" he said.

"We've come about the apples," said Mr Fooby-Lartil.

"What apples?" said Mr Grimbott.

"Yours," said Mrs Fooby-Lartil. "We were wondering . . ."

"No, you can't," snapped Mr Grimbott. "We're much too poor. We need all of them. We can't afford to give any away."

"We weren't asking you to *give* them to us," said Mr Fooby-Lartil.

"Well, you certainly can't afford to pay," said Mr Grimbott.

"Everybody knows you don't have any money at all," said Mrs Grimbott, appearing in the hall behind him. "You ought to get proper jobs and stop messing round with those foolish inventions of yours. You can't expect us to look after you."

"We don't," said Mrs Fooby-Lartil, managing to keep her temper with some difficulty.

"What we wondered," said Mr Fooby-Lartil, "was whether you might be interested in a swap."

"What kind of a swap?"

"A scarecrow," said Mr Fooby-Lartil. He waved towards the apple trees where the crows were wheeling and circling. "To scare them off," he explained.

"Hmm," said Mr Grimbott. "Wait a minute." He went back inside the house with Mrs Grimbott.

"What are you talking about?" hissed Percy.

"Sssh," said Mrs Fooby-Lartil. "We'll tell you later."

The Grimbotts came back.

"We've decided," said Mr Grimbott, "that you can come and pick up the windfalls. But you can't take any off the trees."

"And mind you come when it's dark," said Mrs Grimbott. "We don't want people to think you're visiting us."

"Humph," said Percy.

"Your cat just said 'Humph'," said Mrs Grimbott, staring at Percy.

"He sneezed!"   "He choked!"

          said Mr and Mrs Fooby-Lartil together.

"It sounded to me as if he was speaking,"

said Mrs Grimbott, still gazing at Percy.

Percy sat down and began to wash behind his ears.

"A speaking cat," said Mr Fooby-Lartil. "I don't think that's possible. Now about those apples . . ."

"Not a single one till you've brought us the scarecrow," said Mr Grimbott.

Mrs Fooby-Lartil was dismayed. "Please," she said, "couldn't we have just two or three to be going on with?"

"Certainly not!" said Mrs Grimbott. "We told you already. We can't afford to give them away."

"Well, we'd better be getting on," said Mr Fooby-Lartil. "The sooner we start on the scarecrow, the sooner we get fed."

"Quite right," said Mrs Grimbott.

"And make sure it's a good quality scarecrow," called Mr Grimbott as they set off down the path. "We don't want any old rubbish."

He banged his front door shut.

* * *

"Rude!" said Percy as they turned in at their own gate. "I don't want any of their rotten old fruit. I'd rather go without."

"Take no notice," said Mr Fooby-Lartil. "We're too poor. We need the apples. Don't let it get to you, Percy."

"Charity," said Percy. "I don't want charity."

"Don't worry," said Mrs Fooby-Lartil. "We're inventing a scarecrow for them to keep the birds off their apples. That's a fair exchange, not charity."

And she went whistling off to start on the scarecrow.

"I wish she wouldn't whistle like that," said Percy. "It gives me a headache."

"Doing the washing-up's a great cure for a headache," said Mr Fooby-Lartil.

"Very funny," said Percy witheringly. "And anyway, she's supposed to be finishing her Self-Making Bed."

"She's going to," said Mr Fooby-Lartil. "But she's making the scarecrow first. Now what about seeing if you can find an onion or some carrots and I'll go and pick the last few blackberries."

"Blackberry and onions," said Percy, pulling a face.

Mr Fooby-Lartil pretended not to notice.

"When I think of that awful Persian at the Grimbotts' getting cream and mackerel every day," moaned Percy, "I feel sick. It's not fair. Cream and mackerel! For that great fat thing. I ask you, is that justice?"

"You never know, you might find a bit of mackerel or some fish heads round the back of the fish and chip shop," suggested Mr Fooby-Lartil.

"The Grimbotts' cat gets hers out of a tin," said Percy enviously.

"Try asking her for a taste," said Mr Fooby-Lartil.

"Humph!" said Percy, flouncing out of the gate.

Chapter 7

It took Mrs Fooby-Lartil nearly a week to make the scarecrow. By the time it was ready, the Fooby-Lartils and Percy were so thin and weak from eating only blackberries and the occasional carrot and potato, they could hardly find enough strength to carry it over to the Grimbotts'.

"Why can't it walk?" asked Percy.

"I didn't programme it to walk," said Mrs Fooby-Lartil. "It doesn't need to. All it has to do is stand and wave its arms and shout, 'Shoo! Go away!' "

"If you'd programmed it to walk," said Percy, "it could move round the orchard waving."

"It's not as easy as that," said Mrs Fooby-Lartil. "It might walk into trees or trip over."

"I think it looks very ferocious," said Mr Fooby-Lartil. "If I were a crow, it'd scare me."

He took hold of the scarecrow's legs and swung them up over his shoulder. "You take the head," he told his wife. "It's lighter. And Percy can prop up the back."

Percy stretched out his paws.

"Don't bump the control panel, will you?" said Mrs Fooby-Lartil.

As she spoke, Percy slipped on the path and fell. Ping! His paw hit a button in the

scarecrow's back. "Stone the crows!" it shouted. "Shoo! Go away!"

Percy gave a loud yowl and leapt back.

"It's all right," said Mrs Fooby-Lartil. "You hit the talking button, that's all. But try not to do it again."

Percy took a look at the buttons. "D'you want to know what they say?" said Mr Fooby-Lartil.

Percy threw him a huffy look. "I can read perfectly well, thank you," he said. He looked at the panel. "Hmm," he said. "I see."

"Can you push the DELAY button, please?" said Mrs Fooby-Lartil from behind the scarecrow's head. "That'll keep it quiet till we get there."

Percy took a look at the buttons.

"W . . A . . V . . E . . . That must be DELAY," he thought. "Definitely. It's the biggest button." He pushed it. Then, to be sure he hadn't got it wrong, he pressed T A L K and M O V E and for good measure, the little one on the side that said D E L A Y.

"Have you done it?" Mrs Fooby-Lartil's

voice came floating out from behind the scarecrow's old hat.

"Just finished," said Percy hurriedly. He glanced anxiously at the scarecrow. It wasn't moving, so he must have got the buttons right. He heaved a sigh of relief.

"Okay," called Mr Fooby-Lartil from under the feet. "Prop up the back there, Percy, and we're away."

The Grimbotts were pleased with the scarecrow.

"Good," said Mr Grimbott. "I'm glad to see you've made something useful for a change."

"Let's put it in the orchard right away," said Mrs Grimbott. "It'll stop the crows stealing the apples. And it might scare off children, too."

"I'd have thought you had enough apples to spare for children," said Mrs Fooby-Lartil.

"Not at all," said Mrs Grimbott. "You can never have too many apples."

They took the scarecrow into the orchard and set it in place.

"How does it work?" asked Mrs Grimbott.

"Watch," said Mrs Fooby-Lartil, going behind it and punching some of the buttons.

For a few minutes, the scarecrow did nothing. Then it slowly began to shake its head. As they watched, it opened its mouth, threw back its head, gave a loud shriek and waved its arms wildly. The crows which had been circling the apples, flapped away. The Grimbotts were impressed. "It's better than I thought it'd be," said Mr Grimbott grudgingly.

"You can come tonight and pick up some fallen apples," said Mrs Grimbott. "But don't take too many. We might need them."

Percy snorted.

So for the next few weeks the Fooby-Lartils had apple cake, apple sauce, apple tart, apple pudding, apple turnovers, apple juice, apple tea, apple pie, stewed apple, baked apple, boiled apple, fried apple, apple fritters, apple pancakes, apple porridge and apple soup.

"I told you I can do anything with an

apple," said Mr Fooby-Lartil proudly.

"Apple and fish heads, apple and mouse," said Percy. "What a diet. Compared with some cats I know." But he took care to say it where Mr Fooby-Lartil couldn't hear him.

And, "Better than no food at all," said Mrs Fooby-Lartil in a resigned tone.

But about a week later, the Fooby-Lartils woke up to loud screams. "That sounds like Mr Grimbott," said Mrs Fooby-Lartil. "I wonder what's the matter."

"Quick!" shrieked Mr Grimbott. "Help! Police!"

Out rushed the Fooby-Lartils in their pyjamas. "What's the matter?" cried Mrs Fooby-Lartil.

"The scarecrow," panted Mr Grimbott. "It's gone mad. It's going all over the orchard biting apples and throwing them everywhere. And it's screaming and shrieking and trying to attack us."

The Fooby-Lartils raced to the orchard. The scarecrow was walking stiffly from tree to tree, pulling off apples, taking a bite out of each,

then throwing them on the grass.

"Look at that," moaned Mr Grimbott. "What a waste. What a mess."

Mr and Mrs Fooby-Lartil seized the scarecrow by its clothing and tried to pull it away. "Shoo!" screamed the scarecrow, hitting at them with its wooden arms. "Get away! Keep off! Stone the crows!"

It crashed sideways into one of the apple trees, bounced off and staggered on. "Get lost, you ugly critters! Go away!" it shrieked. "Pests! Thieves!"

Mrs Fooby-Lartil stalked it for several minutes, then did a low rugby tackle and brought it crashing to the ground.

Mr Fooby-Lartil whipped off his pyjama pants and tied its wooden hands together, then stopped its bellowing by popping a large apple into its mouth.

"Stand clear of its legs," he warned as he hoisted it in a fireman's lift over his shoulders and strode home.

Mr Grimbott was purple with rage. "Did you see that?" he demanded. "What does he think he's doing? It's disgraceful. It's out-rageous. Walking in my orchard *with no trousers on*."

"He's only trying to help," said Mrs Fooby-Lartil. "What else can he do?"

"Make a proper scarecrow that doesn't go wrong," said Mr Grimbott. "Useless thing." He looked around him. "It'll take me all day to clean this up," he said. "No more apples for you. And keep out of my orchard from now on. You're lucky I haven't called the police."

Mrs Fooby-Lartil went sadly home. "We're back to square one," she said. "But the blackberries are over now. What are we going to eat?"

Chapter 8

Around lunchtime, when the Fooby-Lartils'
cuckoo clock had called twenty-seven and then
twelve, there was a scuffling at the back door
and the sound of something heavy being
dragged along. Mr Fooby-Lartil opened the
door. "Percy!" he cried. "Whatever have you
got there?"

Percy let go of what he was pulling. "A joint
of lamb," he said. "For lunch."

"Roast lamb," said Mrs Fooby-Lartil, "My
mouth's watering already. But where did you
find it?"

Percy looked awkward. "Oh, just around,"
he said. "Someone didn't want it any more, so

I brought it home. It's taken me ages," he added, looking meaningly at the large chunk of meat. "And I've hardly eaten any on the way."

"But why?" said Mrs Fooby-Lartil. "You haven't found any food for ages and suddenly you go out and bring back all this. You are wonderful, Percy."

She went over and hugged him. Percy looked sheepish. "Oh well," he said. "It's nothing really."

"It's my turn to cook," said Mrs Fooby-Lartil. "I'll go and start on the lamb right away. You're a marvel, Percy."

Mr Fooby-Lartil waited till she'd been gone for a few minutes. "You know those buttons on the scarecrow's control panel, Percy," he said. "You didn't fiddle with them by any chance, did you?"

"Me!" said Percy indignantly. "What a thing to say. And after all the trouble I've gone to. As if I would."

He sat down, offended, and began to wash behind his ears.

Mr Fooby-Lartil sucked on his pipe for a

while, then he said casually, "Would you mind passing me that book over there please?"

"Which one?" said Percy.

"*New Inventions*," said Mr Fooby-Lartil. "The blue one."

Percy looked at the shelf. There were five blue books. He gazed at the letters on the covers. "BCHSIKQP," he read silently. "WQRTUUNMOP," "VVMKPTS," "PPTS", "FFTSPPLOB." Yes that must be it. That one—WQRTUUNMOP. It looked important, the way Percy thought an invention book should look. He took it down and gave it to Mr Fooby-Lartil. "Here you are," he said carelessly.

"Thanks," said Mr Fooby-Lartil. "Maybe you could give a hand in the kitchen if you're free. I'll come and set the table in a minute."

"Right," said Percy, pleased his reading had been so successful. He trotted off to help.

Mr Fooby-Lartil put *How to Look After Your Rabbit* back onto the bookshelf. He grinned to himself. "Poor old Percy," he thought. "But never mind. Roast lamb's a lot more filling than baked apple. And much tastier."

And he bounced off to the kitchen, his mouth watering in anticipation.

chapter 9

"Good news," said Mrs Fooby-Lartil as she took the roast lamb out of the oven.

"Yes?" said the others.

"I've finished my Self-Making Bed," she said. She put the roasting pan on the table. "If we can find someone to buy it, our troubles'll be over."

There was a bang from behind her as the Cupboard slammed its doors. "I said the Self-Making Bed, not the Self-Stacking Cupboard," said Mrs Fooby-Lartil.

"So pipe down," said Percy rudely.

The Cupboard made a grinding noise. "Now you've done it," said Mr Fooby-Lartil. "It's locked itself."

"Stupid Cupboard," said Percy.

"It's not stupid," said Mr Fooby-Lartil. "It's very useful."

"Could you get the plates out for me please, Percy?" said Mrs Fooby-Lartil.

"It won't let me," said Percy, struggling with the key.

"Here," said Mr Fooby-Lartil. "I'll try." He wrenched the key round in the lock, then pulled hard on the doorknobs but the Cupboard stubbornly gripped its doors tight shut.

"Come on, Cupboard," said Mr Fooby-Lartil, stroking the top of it. "There's a good Cupboard. Let's have the plates now."

The Cupboard shook itself and a cup fell onto Mr Fooby-Lartil's head. "Ow!" he cried and kicked the doors.

"Now we'll *never* get anything out of it," said Percy gloomily. "We'll have to put the dinner on my saucer. Why can't we have a normal cupboard?"

"Think of the work it saves us," said Mrs Fooby-Lartil. "We never have to put the

dishes away. It does it all for us."

"*Us*," said Percy. "What do you mean, 'us'? I do all the housework round here. You two are always much too busy."

"That's not true," said Mr Fooby-Lartil. "I washed the dishes just last night."

"Pretty feeble job too," said Percy. "You were half-blind from that explosion in your shed and you left dirt all over them. That's another reason that Cupboard's in a huff. It doesn't like storing dirty dishes."

"Was there another explosion?" said Mrs Fooby-Lartil. "I didn't hear anything."

Percy looked accusing. "You had your old rock and roll records on at top volume, that's why," he said.

"My Troublefree-Teamaker blew up again," said Mr Fooby-Lartil. "But there's only a tiny hole in the shed roof. And I've cracked it this time. It was the boiling valve."

Percy sighed. "This is a madhouse," he said. "I'm hungry. I want my share of the lamb." He shot the Fooby-Lartils a nasty look. "I'm sorry to have to remind you," he said, "but I *was* the one who found it."

"Just give the Cupboard a few more minutes," said Mrs Fooby-Lartil, "then it'll be all right."

Mr Fooby-Lartil looked at the cuckoo clock. Mrs Fooby-Lartil had always wanted a cuckoo clock. "That's the best thing about being an inventor," she was fond of saying. "Whatever you want you can invent." The clock was shaped like a little wooden house with a door where the cuckoo came out every hour. But the Fooby-Lartils' cuckoo was not very good at counting. As Mr Fooby-Lartil watched, it popped out of the clock, called "Cuckoo!" fourteen times, then slammed the door.

"Heavens. Fourteen o'clock already," said Mrs Fooby-Lartil. "We must eat soon."

"We can't," said Percy. "That stupid Cupboard won't let us. You ought to sell it. You don't need it. I can put away the dishes much better than that old Cupboard any day."

"That's true, you know," said Mr Fooby-Lartil thoughtfully. Instantly the Cupboard gave a creak and its doors sprang open.

"Thanks," said Mrs Fooby-Lartil, reaching inside for three plates. She piled them up with roast lamb.

"What a feast," said Mr Fooby-Lartil. "Thank you, Percy. This is wonderful."

Percy looked modest. "It's nothing," he said. "Well, almost nothing . . . that is, I mean . . . it *was* quite a hard job finding it. And dangerous, of course. I risked my life really, bringing it home. But I don't mind. No, I don't mind at all." He took a large mouthful and chewed on it happily.

"Where *did* you find it?" asked Mr Fooby-Lartil.

Percy choked on his lamb. "Oh . . . just about," he said carelessly.

"About where?" said Mrs Fooby-Lartil.

"Here and there."

"Here and there where?" said Mr Fooby-Lartil.

Percy thought for a minute. Then, "Up a tree," he said. "Yes, that's where. Up a very tall tree. A walnut tree, I think it was. It just flew into the branches and I raced up the tree and caught it before it could fly away."

The Fooby-Lartils looked at each other.

"Lamb comes from a young sheep," said Mrs Fooby-Lartil. "And sheep don't fly. So you don't find them up trees."

"This one must have been able to fly," said Percy. "It was definitely up a tree."

"Are you sure it wasn't a gum tree?" asked Mr Fooby-Lartil sarcastically.

"It might have been," said Percy. "But on the other hand, it might not."

Mrs Fooby-Lartil stared very hard at Percy. Percy went on concentrating on his lamb. "I'm sorry to have to ask you this," she said, "but are you quite sure you didn't steal it?"

"Me!" shrieked Percy. "Steal food!" He pointed an accusing paw at Mr Fooby-Lartil. "That's what he does!" he shouted. "Taking all those apples from the Grimbotts' orchard."

"*Did* you steal it?" asked Mr Fooby-Lartil.

"No, I did not," said Percy huffily. "I didn't steal it off the Grimbotts' table while they were out and I wish you'd stop saying I did."

He threw Mr Fooby-Lartil a nasty look. "If you go on accusing me like that," he said, "I just might leave home."

Mr Fooby-Lartil winked at Mrs Fooby-Lartil over his plate of lamb. "We'd be sorry to lose you, Percy," he said, "but I suppose you could always go and live at the Grimbotts'. I'm sure they could do with another good mouser."

"Excuse *me*," said Percy haughtily. He got up from the table, picked up his half-finished plate and stalked out into the garden.

"There's no pleasing some people," they heard him mutter as he went.

Mrs Fooby-Lartil looked crossly at her husband. "Now you've done it," she said. "That wasn't very clever. Or very kind. He meant to be helpful. And what about the lamb? What'll we do if the Grimbotts suspect and come looking for it?"

Mr Fooby-Lartil gobbled down another thick slice. "Eat it up quick," he said. "Without any evidence, they can't prove a thing."

And he picked up another piece on his fork and started to eat that too.

Chapter 10

Percy was sitting in the garden washing himself when Mrs Fooby-Lartil came out.

"I want your advice on my new inventions," she said. "By the way, I'm sorry about that business with the lamb. It was delicious. And very kind of you."

"That's all right," said Percy stiffly. "I don't hold you responsible. It's him again. He's got it in for me. He's jealous."

"Oh, Percy," said Mrs Fooby-Lartil. "Of course he's not. He's just as fond of you as I am."

"Huh!" said Percy, but Mrs Fooby-Lartil noticed he looked pleased.

"You know," said Mrs Fooby-Lartil kindly, "even if someone was very hungry it wouldn't be right to take food from someone else without asking."

Percy examined his paw. "I suppose not," he said. "What's that advice you wanted?"

"It's my new inventions," said Mrs Fooby-Lartil. "I need your opinion."

Percy looked pleased.

"I'm working on a Remote-Control-Pencil," said Mrs Fooby-Lartil, "and the World's-First-Waterproof-Banana-Peeler."

"How does a waterproof banana-peeler work?" asked Percy, puzzled.

"Like this," said Mrs Fooby-Lartil, pulling out a drawing from a pocket in her white coat.

"I see," said Percy. "You shut the umbrella and the banana gets peeled."

"D'you think it's a good idea?" said Mrs Fooby-Lartil.

"Very good," said Percy. "What about the pencil?"

"The Remote-Control-Pencil," said Mrs Fooby-Lartil, "helps you with your work. You

Waterproof Banana Peeler

fig 1

Banana

String

Stout Umbrella

fig 2

Peeled

Umbrella folded

©Mr Foby-L'art.1

can be in one place and the pencil can be writing for you somewhere else. You just tell it what to do."

"How?" said Percy.

From another pocket, Mrs Fooby-Lartil pulled out a small box like a television remote control unit. Then she took out a large silver pencil. She placed the pencil point-down on the back of the paper with the drawing of the Banana-Peeler. "Watch," she said.

She let go of the pencil and spoke into the remote control unit. "Today is Tuesday," she said. All by itself, the pencil neatly wrote: *Today is Tuesday*. "In capitals, please," said Mrs Fooby-Lartil to the remote control unit. *TODAY IS TUESDAY*, wrote the pencil.

"You try," said Mrs Fooby-Lartil, handing the unit to Percy. Percy gingerly set the pencil on its point and took hold of the remote control unit. "Press that button," said Mrs Fooby-Lartil. "Then let it go again."

Percy pressed the button. "Mice!" he said gruffly.

Mice! wrote the pencil.

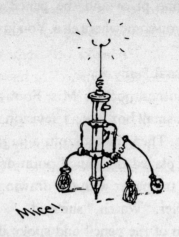

Mice!

Percy examined the writing. "It says Mice," he announced.

"Yes," said Mrs Fooby-Lartil.

"I can see that," said Percy, still holding the remote control button. "I can read."

I can see that, wrote the pencil. *I can read.*

Percy looked at the new writing. "Yes, mice," he said again.

Yes, mice, wrote the pencil.

"I think it might be a good idea to let go of the button," said Mrs Fooby-Lartil. "Well, what do you think?"

"It's a good idea," said Percy, "but I still think those shampoo pads for the paws I mentioned . . ." He broke off. Someone was coming in at the gate. "Oh no," he hissed. "Oh help! It's the Grimbotts."

And before Mrs Fooby-Lartil could stop him, he leapt up the pine tree to the topmost branch and disappeared amongst the foliage.

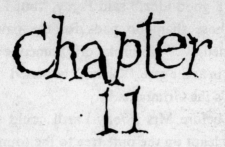

Chapter 11

Mr Grimbott shook his fist at Mrs Fooby-Lartil. "Thief!" he shouted. "Pilferer!"

Mrs Fooby-Lartil glanced at the pine tree. Percy was nowhere to be seen. "I'm afraid I don't know what you're talking about," she said.

"Oh yes you do," cried Mr Grimbott. "Stealing our dinner from right under our noses. How dare you!"

He marched up the path towards the house.

"Now we're for it," thought Mrs Fooby-Lartil. "If he sees the remains of the lamb on the table we're in real trouble."

She had just started to follow Mr Grimbott

when she realised Mrs Grimbott was standing by the gate gazing up at the pine tree. "And I don't like the look on her face," said Mrs Fooby-Lartil to herself. "I hope she didn't hear Percy talking."

Mr Grimbott was beating on the door. Out came Mr Fooby-Lartil. "Yes?" he said. "What do you want?"

"I want my dinner back, that's what I want," bellowed Mr Grimbott.

Mrs Grimbott came up the path. "Don't you deny it," she said. "I'd just put it on the table to cool when you called, 'Fire! Fire!'"

"You knew we'd rush out," said Mr Grimbott.

"And then you seized your chance," went on Mrs Grimbott. "You raced inside, snatched it off the dish and by the time we got back you'd made off with it."

"Give it back right now," cried Mr Grimbott, "or I'll get the law on you."

"Just a minute," said Mr Fooby-Lartil. "This is a very serious matter. You say I stole your dinner."

"I certainly do," said Mr Grimbott. "A succulent leg of best lamb."

"And then you say I made off home with it?"

"Yes," said Mrs Grimbott.

"How?" said Mr Fooby-Lartil. "Even supposing I'd stolen it, and I assure you I didn't, how could I get it back here without you seeing me?"

"I don't know what you mean," said Mr Grimbott, a little more quietly.

"There's only one path going up to your house," said Mr Fooby-Lartil. "One way in and one way out. You couldn't have missed seeing me. If I'd been there. Which I wasn't."

"You could've gone over the orchard wall," said Mrs Grimbott.

"In broad daylight?" said Mr Fooby-Lartil.

"You'd have seen him then too," pointed out Mrs Fooby-Lartil.

The Grimbotts looked at each other. "Are you saying you didn't take that joint?" asked Mr Grimbott.

"I certainly am," said Mr Fooby-Lartil. "And my wife didn't take it either. We had nothing at all to do with stealing your dinner."

Mrs Fooby-Lartil felt uncomfortable. It was true they hadn't stolen the lamb but they had eaten it.

"It's not as if we realised," she told herself. "Well, not till it was too late anyway."

"Come in," said Mr Fooby-Lartil. "See for yourself."

Mrs Fooby-Lartil looked at him in horror. The Grimbotts would see the remains of their dinner on the table and that would be that. As she followed him in, she noticed Percy slinking quietly towards the house below the hedge.

With a sinking heart she went indoors. But the table was nearly bare. Only a crust of bread and a jar with a scraping of marmalade were sitting on it.

"There," said Mr Fooby-Lartil.

"You've hidden it," said Mr Grimbott, flinging open the pantry door.

Mrs Grimbott looked under the table. Her husband looked behind the curtains. "Nothing but a lot of dust there," he said and sneezed.

"Excuse *me*," said Percy from the doorway.

"I dusted just last week."

Mrs Fooby-Lartil pulled a terrible face at Percy. "Just last week," she repeated in a voice as much like Percy's as she could manage.

"That cat spoke," said Mrs Grimbott. "I heard it."

Mr Fooby-Lartil threw back his head and laughed. "That was Mrs Fooby-Lartil," he said. "And it's very rude to tell her she's got a cat's voice."

"I heard it," said Mrs Grimbott. "With my own ears."

"Of course you didn't," said her husband. "Don't be ridiculous. They're trying to put you off looking for our stolen dinner."

"I keep telling you we didn't steal it," said Mr Fooby-Lartil. "If you think we took it, where is it then?"

Mr Grimbott looked round. "There," he said triumphantly, pointing at the Cupboard. Mrs Fooby-Lartil's heart sank.

"That cupboard," said Mr Fooby-Lartil scornfully. "Useless thing. You can't even get the doors open."

"I'm going to open it right now," said Mr Grimbott, "and prove you've taken our food."

He went over to the Cupboard and hauled on the key. It was stuck fast. He twisted and wrenched but the key wouldn't budge. With Mrs Grimbott pulling too, he dragged on the doors and tried in vain to prise them open.

"You see?" said Mr Fooby-Lartil. "It's been stuck like that ever since we've had it."

Mr Grimbott looked embarrassed.

"It's a very serious matter, accusing someone unjustly of theft," said Mr Fooby-Lartil. "If I were a meaner man I'd go down to the Town Hall and complain to the Mayor."

Mrs Grimbott turned pale. "We were just joking," she said. "There's no need to go to the Mayor."

"Not much of a joke for us," said Mr Fooby-Lartil.

"I'll bring you some apples," said Mr Grimbott. "To make up."

Percy was sitting on a chair behind the Grimbotts.

"You ought to apologise," he said sternly. "Say sorry."

The Grimbotts swung round. "That cat's talking again," said Mrs Grimbott. "I told you."

"Yes," said Mrs Fooby-Lartil in her strange combination voice. "Say you're sorry. Apologise please."

"Why's she talking like that?" demanded Mrs Grimbott.

"She's got hayfever," said Mr Fooby-Lartil hastily.

Mrs Fooby-Lartil nodded.

"In Autumn?" said Mr Grimbott.

"Lots of people get it in Autumn. From the leaves," said Mr Fooby-Lartil.

Mrs Fooby-Lartil nodded again. She wished they would hurry up and leave. And when she got her hands on Percy . . .

"I might just pop down to the Town Hall," said Mr Fooby-Lartil. "Maybe I should have a word with the Mayor."

"We'll be on our way now," said Mr Grimbott hurriedly, pushing his wife out of the door. "Sorry about that little mix-up."

And they went off down the path.

But from inside the house, the Fooby-Lartils could hear Mrs Grimbott saying as they went, "I *did* hear their cat talking. I tell you I did."

Chapter 12

"Right," said Mrs Fooby-Lartil. "The time has come for a serious talk." She sat down next to Percy. "Look at all the trouble that's come from taking something that didn't belong to us."

"I didn't know they were going to come round here," said Percy indignantly.

"But it was their food," said Mrs Fooby-Lartil. "So really we shouldn't have had it at all. I know you meant to be helpful, Percy, and we're very grateful, but we can't take things that aren't ours."

"Why not?" said Percy. "We haven't got any and they've got lots."

"They don't see it like that," said Mrs Fooby-Lartil.

"It was delicious, wasn't it?" said Percy, his eyes gleaming at the remembrance of the roast lamb.

"Very good," said Mr Fooby-Lartil. "And there's enough over for tonight." He patted the Cupboard, the key turned in the lock and the doors sprang open. There sat the dish with the remains of the lamb.

"Maybe we should return it," said Mrs Fooby-Lartil.

"Of course we can't," said Mr Fooby-Lartil. "Not now. But you mustn't ever do that again, Percy."

Percy sighed.

"I know you meant to be helpful," said Mrs Fooby-Lartil. "Never mind."

"There's another thing, too," said Mr Fooby-Lartil. "You mustn't let anyone else hear you talking."

"Why not?" said Percy.

"Too dangerous," said Mr Fooby-Lartil.

"I hardly said anything," said Percy.

"Cheek, he's got. Dust indeed."

"You shouldn't say a word in front of other people," explained Mrs Fooby-Lartil.

"Oh wonderful," said Percy. "First they turn me into a talking freak, then they tell me not to speak. Marvellous. Very helpful. Maybe I should just wear a gag."

"Well, now you come to mention it . . ." began Mr Fooby-Lartil.

"Of course not," broke in Mrs Fooby-Lartil. "Don't be silly. It's just that we don't want you to get into any trouble."

Percy drew himself up. "I can look after myself perfectly well, thank you," he said frostily. He glowered at Mr Fooby-Lartil. "Unlike some people I could mention. Always blowing things up. Serving other people with blackberry and mouse and expecting them to eat it. Ungrateful when you risk your life to get them a decent meal. I've a good mind to leave home." His tail quivered with indignation as he walked out. "And by the way," he said nastily, pausing in the doorway, "there's a hole in your shirt, in case you haven't noticed. A great big huge one. It's a disgrace. You ought to be ashamed of yourself."

He slammed out.

Mr Fooby-Lartil mopped his brow. "Thank goodness he's gone," he said. "I could do with some peace and quiet."

"I'm going for a nice long walk in the woods," said Mrs Fooby-Lartil. "D'you want to come?"

"No thanks," said Mr Fooby-Lartil. "I'll get back to my Teamaker. It's almost finished. I think I've really cracked it this time."

Chapter 13

When Mr Fooby-Lartil came in from the shed, Percy was sitting in his favourite armchair, gazing at a book.

"Hello," said Mr Fooby-Lartil.

"Ssshh," said Percy. "I'm reading."

Mr Fooby-Lartil decided it would be unkind to tell Percy he was holding the book upside-down. "Enjoying it?" he said instead.

Percy nodded. "It's about this cat who lives in a palace," he said. "He gets cream and mackerel to eat every day."

"I see," said Mr Fooby-Lartil who could read upside-down and had already noticed the book's title was *A Life on the Ocean Wave*.

"Any boats in it?"

"Boats?" said Percy. "In a palace? Don't be silly." He went on reading.

"Mrs Fooby-Lartil's not home yet?"

"I haven't seen her," said Percy.

"She went for a walk in the woods ages ago," said Mr Fooby-Lartil. He looked at the cuckoo clock. Quarter past twenty-five. Outside it was getting dark. "She ought to be back by now," he said.

"If she's not back for dinner," said Percy, "that'll mean all the more roast lamb for us two."

"That's not very nice," said Mr Fooby-Lartil.

An hour later, Mrs Fooby-Lartil still had not returned. By now, Mr Fooby-Lartil was very worried indeed. Percy had given up reading and had climbed the pine tree three times to see if he could spot her.

"Something must have happened to her," he said in a small voice. "I hope no one's thrown her in the pond."

Mr Fooby-Lartil noticed he was shivering. "I'm sure she's just delayed," he said kindly. "You stay here in case she gets back and I'll go out with the Torch and try to find her."

"I'd rather come and help you," said Percy humbly. "She might have twisted her ankle or something and be lying on the ground."

"Right," said Mr Fooby-Lartil. "Let's get our coats on and get started."

He pulled on his old tweed coat while Percy

struggled into his woollen one. Once it had been a legwarmer of Mrs Fooby-Lartil's but she had given it to Percy when he admired its red and purple stripes. He pulled the second-best teacosy over his ears to keep them warm and watched Mr Fooby-Lartil get out the Encouraging-Torch. As he switched it on, the Torch began to shout cheerfully, "Nearly there. Almost arrived. Just about home now."

Percy was puzzled. "What's it on about?" he said. "We are home. We haven't gone yet."

"You're supposed to use it when you're out and coming home," explained Mr Fooby-Lartil. "It keeps you going when you think you can't manage to walk any more."

They set off together towards the woods. Percy slipped his paw into Mr Fooby-Lartil's hand. "*I'm* not scared of the dark," he said. "But you'd better hold my paw in case you get frightened."

"Thanks," said Mr Fooby-Lartil.

Percy pressed up close to him. "It's a lot darker in these woods than you'd expect," he said.

Mr Fooby-Lartil swung the Torch from side to side. The beam of light lit up the trees but there was no sign of Mrs Fooby-Lartil anywhere. "I suppose," said Percy, clutching Mr Fooby-Lartil's hand even tighter, "it'd be a good idea for me to climb up one of those trees."

"No need," said Mr Fooby-Lartil. "We're better to stick together."

Percy heaved a sigh of relief.

They had hunted and called for Mrs Fooby-Lartil for nearly half an hour and were on the point of going back home when Percy heard a faint sound in the distance. "A sort of grunt," he told Mr Fooby-Lartil.

"Hello! Over here!" they shouted together.

And suddenly a familiar voice called back faintly, "It's me! Is that you?"

"Yes," cried Mr Fooby-Lartil. "Thank goodness we've found you."

They raced towards the voice and saw Mrs Fooby-Lartil stumbling through the trees. She was overjoyed to see them. "I didn't think I'd be able to find my way home," she said.

"Thank goodness you came to look for me."

"We were worried you might have gone for good," said Mr Fooby-Lartil, as they set off homewards.

"I got delayed," said Mrs Fooby-Lartil. "And then it got dark suddenly and I couldn't find the path. I must say that Torch's light is very comforting."

"Nearly there," shouted the Torch.

"It's been doing that ever since we left," said Percy. "You can't believe a word it says."

Mrs Fooby-Lartil laughed. "We are nearly home this time," she said. "See. There's the gate."

"Something's making a funny noise," said Mr Fooby-Lartil as they trooped into the bright warm kitchen.

"And something smells *awful*," said Percy, sniffing.

"That's why I was late," said Mrs Fooby-Lartil. "Look." She took her hand away from her pocket. The pocket quivered and out peeped a tiny little nose.

"Eek!" screeched Percy. "It's alive! What is it?"

"A piglet," said Mrs Fooby-Lartil. "A very small one. I found him squealing in the woods. I've hunted everywhere for his mother but I can't find her."

"Let me see," said Mr Fooby-Lartil, putting out his hand. The pocket shook again and the nose vanished.

"He's terrified," said Mrs Fooby-Lartil. "I've wrapped him in my handkerchief to keep him warm."

She reached down into her pocket and drew the piglet out. He flattened his ears back against his head and squealed.

"You're all right," said Mr Fooby-Lartil.

Mrs Fooby-Lartil stroked his head. "He's very young," she said. "We'll have to hand feed him for a while."

Mr Fooby-Lartil sighed. "It's a nuisance," he said.

"But I couldn't just leave him there on his own," said Mrs Fooby-Lartil.

"Of course not," agreed Mr Fooby-Lartil.

"It's making your pocket really pongy," said Percy, taking a sniff. "Yukkk! That's what the smell was. Why don't you take it back where you found it?"

Mrs Fooby-Lartil went to the drawer and took out some scissors. With two quick snips she made an airhole at the bottom of her pocket, then cut the handkerchief to make some nappies, fastened them on the piglet and popped him back into her pocket again.

"He can stay there till he's a bit older," she said.

"Spoilt little brat," said Percy, just loudly enough to be heard.

"That's nasty, Percy," said Mr Fooby-Lartil. "You're jealous."

"*Me*?" said Percy. "*Jealous*! That's a laugh. Me! I wouldn't want to go round in her pocket. Not if she invited me."

"Put a sock in it, Percy," said Mr Fooby-Lartil.

"Don't be mean," said Mrs Fooby-Lartil. "Be kind to him. He's only a baby."

"Some baby," snorted Percy.

"You are jealous," said Mrs Fooby-Lartil.

"Of that dirty thing," said Percy scornfully. "Huh. Not me. And it's not having any of my lamb either."

Chapter 14

The Fooby-Lartils and Percy finished up the lamb. The piglet was now fast asleep in Mrs Fooby-Lartil's pocket.

"I'm going to bed," said Percy. "I'm sure no one's noticed and no one cares but I've had a long and tiring day."

"You've been magnificent," said Mrs Fooby-Lartil. "We're really grateful."

She looked at the empty plate where the lamb had been. "What a feast," she said. "We won't want to eat for several days after this."

"I will," said Percy. "I'll want to eat tomorrow, the way they do in a normal household."

"I'll see what there is for tomorrow," said Mr Fooby-Lartil. He looked in the larder. "There's some porridge," he said. "We could have that for tomorrow's dinner. I'll mix it up now and let it brew overnight."

"Good idea," said Mrs Fooby-Lartil, pretending not to notice Percy was pulling a face. "But there's no milk. You'll have to make it with water."

"I'll put in whatever I can find," said Mr Fooby-Lartil, and he set to work. Into the pot went mustard, raisins, some cornflake crumbs, salt, pepper, a scraping from the honey jar, tomato sauce and the juice from the lamb plate. He added the porridge and some water and stirred it hard with a big wooden spoon. "There," he said finally.

"I expect it'll be delicious," said Mrs Fooby-Lartil.

"Errrrkk!" said Percy, sniffing at the pot and turning away in disgust. "But I suppose," he went on, "as long as that stupid piglet gets enough to eat, no one else counts."

He gave a swipe with his paw at the tiny nose

peeping from Mrs Fooby-Lartil's pocket. There was a squeal and cry and the pocket shook.

"*Percy!*" cried the Fooby-Lartils.

"If we don't get some regular food in this house soon," said Percy, "I'm going to eat that piglet."

The pocket grunted. Mrs Fooby-Lartil put her hand inside and stroked the piglet's snout. "Don't worry," she said. "Of course he won't eat you. He's just feeling jealous."

"Oh, jealous, jealous," said Percy. "It's all right for *some* people. Coming in where they're not wanted, swanning round in other people's pockets. Don't mind me. *I* don't care. Some of us have to work, that's all."

And he walked off haughtily.

Two minutes later he was back. "I may be gone for some time," he said darkly. "In fact, you may not see me again ever. I don't believe in hanging around where I'm not wanted." He glared at Mrs Fooby-Lartil's pocket. "Unlike others I could mention."

And he marched outside again.

"It's been a long day," said Mr Fooby-Lartil. "Let's go to bed. Percy'll be all right again in the morning."

Chapter 15

But when the Fooby-Lartils came downstairs next morning, there was no sign of Percy. The piglet, who had slept the night in Mrs Fooby-Lartil's pocket, snuffled round by her feet eating mushed apple from Percy's second-best saucer.

"I wouldn't use that, if I were you," warned Mr Fooby-Lartil. "Not with the mood Percy was in last night."

"I wonder where he is," said Mrs Fooby-Lartil.

"Down at the Grimbotts, I expect," said Mr Fooby-Lartil. "Trying to scrump a bit of mackerel and cream."

It wasn't till lunchtime that Mrs Fooby-Lartil found the note.

"What on earth's that?" said Mr Fooby-Lartil.

"It was on the Cupboard," said Mrs Fooby-Lartil. "I think it's from Percy but I can't work out what it says."

"That's because it doesn't make sense," said Mr Fooby-Lartil. "Look at it."

said the note in large wobbly writing

"He's upset," said Mrs Fooby-Lartil.

"He'll be back," said Mr Fooby-Lartil. "Don't worry about him. He's just being dramatic."

But by late that night, Percy still had not returned.

"What can have happened to him?" said Mrs Fooby-Lartil.

"One night away from home won't hurt him," said Mr Fooby-Lartil.

"Maybe he's really left for good," said Mrs Fooby-Lartil. "I think we should go and look for him."

"But we don't even know where to start," pointed out Mr Fooby-Lartil. "Better to do it tomorrow if he's still not back."

The Fooby-Lartils were up early next morning. They raced down to the kitchen. No Percy. Mrs Fooby-Lartil burst into tears. "I feel terrible," she said. "We shouldn't have been so cross with him."

"He'll turn up," said Mr Fooby-Lartil. "But I'll tell you what, let's go and search for him in the woods. He might have got lost there."

They searched the woods but there was no sign of Percy anywhere. By now Mr Fooby-Lartil was feeling worried too. He went down to the Grimbotts. Mrs Grimbott was in the garden weeding her flower-beds. "You haven't seen our cat, by any chance, have you?" asked Mr Fooby-Lartil.

"If you mean that mangy old thing with half an ear that keeps hanging round here, no I haven't," said Mrs Grimbott.

"If you do see him, will you let us know please?" said Mr Fooby-Lartil.

"I'm sure we won't," said Mrs Grimbott turning her back. "If you ask me, he's gone for good."

Chapter 16

LOST

PERCY FOOBY-LARTIL

Large Tom Cat
with one and a half ears

HANDSOME REWARD
for safe return or information

Three days later, when Percy still had not returned, the Fooby-Lartils put up posters in the town square.

"He might have been run over," said Mrs Fooby-Lartil.

"We'd have heard by now," said Mr Fooby-Lartil but, privately, he too was beginning to wonder if something dreadful had happened.

"What if he starved to death all alone somewhere?" said Mrs Fooby-Lartil. "I feel terrible. We should have been kinder to him."

"We've been very kind to him," said Mr Fooby-Lartil. "Look, worrying about it isn't going to get Percy back. The moon's out and it's quite light. Let's search one last time before bed."

They called as they peered under bushes and hedges and gazed into lighted windows.

"There's no sign of him anywhere," said Mrs Fooby-Lartil.

But just then, she heard a sound in the distance. "Ssh. Listen," she whispered.

This time Mr Fooby-Lartil heard it too.

From far off came a faint familiar yowl. "That's Percy," cried Mrs Fooby-Lartil. "I'm certain of it."

Mr Fooby-Lartil was cautious. "It sounds like him," he said, "but it's hard to be sure."

"Quick. It came from this direction," said Mrs Fooby-Lartil, heading off towards the centre of town.

The yowls grew louder. "That's him all right," said Mr Fooby-Lartil. "But where is he?"

"Percy!" called Mrs Fooby-Lartil.

"Careful," said Mr Fooby-Lartil. "We don't want him to start talking where anyone can hear him."

"I can't work out where the sound's coming from," said Mrs Fooby-Lartil. "It's getting fainter again. We must have passed him. But I don't see where he can be."

"It's almost as if the sound's below us," said Mr Fooby-Lartil.

"That's it!" cried Mrs Fooby-Lartil. "The cells. That's where he is! He's trapped in the cells under the Town Hall."

She hurried towards the barred gratings.

"Percy," she whispered. "Are you there?"

Silence.

"It's me, Percy," she whispered. "We've come to find you."

A loud yowl came up through one of the gratings.

"Over here," hissed Mr Fooby-Lartil. "See. There he is."

"Look at him," said Mrs Fooby-Lartil indignantly. "He's starving. he's so thin. Percy! We're here."

Percy raised his head and stared at them through the bars.

"What happened?" said Mrs Fooby-Lartil.

"I'm dreaming," muttered Percy. "It's not really you."

"It's us all right," said Mr Fooby-Lartil. "What are you doing here?"

"I've been stolen," said Percy. "I've been thieved."

"*Stolen*?" said the Fooby-Lartils. "Who stole you?"

The Grimbotts," said Percy. "I can never come home again. I've been sold. To the Mayor."

"But why?"

Percy looked embarrassed. "They heard me talking," he said. "So they waited till I left home and snatched me and brought me here."

"But why are you in the cells?"

"Because I wouldn't talk," said Percy. "You told me not to talk in front of anyone.

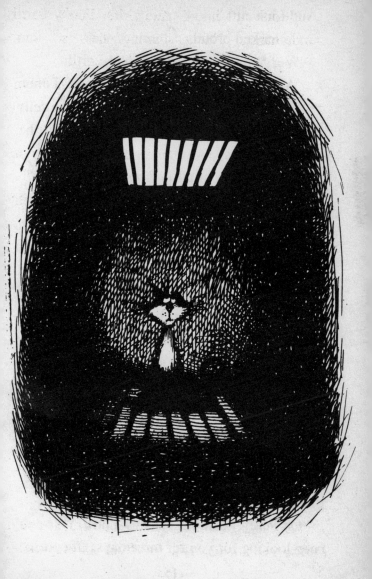

And I haven't."

He looked proud.

"Very good," said Mrs Fooby-Lartil.

"And the Mayor said," went on Percy, "'Right. If he won't talk, put him in the cells with nothing to eat till he decides to be sensible.'"

"Did you talk at all in front of the Mayor?" asked Mr Fooby-Lartil.

"No," said Percy.

"Good," said Mrs Fooby-Lartil. "Now listen carefully. It's too late tonight to do anything but tomorrow morning, we'll go to the Mayor and explain there's been a mistake and get him to let you out."

"But whatever you do," said Mrs Fooby-Lartil, "don't say a word to anyone."

"Not even to us till we get home," warned Mrs Fooby-Lartil.

"You will come back, won't you?" said Percy anxiously. "You won't forget or anything?"

"Oh Percy," said Mrs Fooby-Lartil. "We've been looking for you for three days. Of course we won't forget. We've been so worried."

Percy hung his head. "I didn't really mean what I said in the note," he said.

"We didn't think you did," said Mrs Fooby-Lartil.

"That bit about not coming back ever . . ." said Percy.

"It's all right," said Mr Fooby-Lartil. "We know you didn't mean it. Now try to get some sleep and we'll see you in the morning."

Chapter 17

"I don't believe it," spluttered Mrs Fooby-Lartil as they hurried home. "I didn't think even the Grimbotts would stoop to that. *Selling* Percy."

"And to the Mayor," said Mr Fooby-Lartil. "Everyone knows how horrible he is. Poor Percy. He looks wretched. We'll get him out first thing tomorrow."

"It might not be so easy," said Mrs Fooby-Lartil. "The Mayor will have paid the Grimbotts and he won't be pleased. I don't think he'll give up Percy without a fight."

"Well, we'll see in the morning," said Mr

Fooby-Lartil, yawning. "Let's get some sleep now."

First thing next morning, they hurried off to the Town Hall. The piglet snuggled down in Mrs Fooby-Lartil's pocket, grunting a bit whenever she went over rough ground.

"We want to see the Mayor, please," said Mr Fooby-Lartil.

"Right away," added Mrs Fooby-Lartil. "It's urgent."

"I'll see if I can find him," whispered the Town Clerk. "But I warn you, he was in a terrible mood this morning." He vanished down a long corridor.

Mrs Fooby-Lartil looked round. "It's very impressive," she said. "All these marble floors. And look at the gold leaf on the banisters."

Mr Fooby-Lartil cocked his head. "I think I can hear Percy," he said. "Listen."

"That's not Percy," said Mrs Fooby-Lartil. "It sounds more like a baby crying. Percy's got a much deeper voice than that."

"You're right," said Mr Fooby-Lartil.

"Look, there's the Town Clerk again."

He came scurrying up to them. ("Just like a rat," whispered Mrs Fooby-Lartil.) "The Mayor will see you in ten minutes," he announced grandly. "And please remember to bow when you go into the Mayoral chamber."

"Bow to the Mayor!" said Mr Fooby-Lartil. "Who does he think he is? The king?"

"If you want to keep him in a good mood," said the Town Clerk, "I'd advise you to bow."

"He's too big for his boots, by the sound of it," said Mrs Fooby-Lartil.

"Suit yourselves," said the Town Clerk, as he took them down one corridor, then another and stopped in front of a large silver door. "But don't say I didn't warn you."

Chapter 18

The Town Clerk pushed open the door and the Fooby-Lartils stepped inside the Mayor's office. At the far end of the enormous room, the Mayor sat on a huge golden chair.

"Like a throne," thought Mrs Fooby-Lartil, as they walked towards him over the red carpet. "He really thinks he's important."

"Good morning," said Mr Fooby-Lartil. "We've come about a very urgent matter."

"Most people," said the Mayor, "bow when they meet the Mayor."

"Most mayors," said Mr Fooby-Lartil, "reply when someone says 'good morning' to them." He glowered at the Mayor.

Mrs Fooby-Lartil felt this was a mistake. If the Mayor got angry, he might refuse to give Percy back. Better to keep on the right side of him.

"It's about our cat," she said politely. "He seems to be trapped in the cells under the Town Hall. We went looking for him last night and we heard him yowling down there. So we've come to fetch him."

"Your cat?" said the Mayor. "What do you mean, *your* cat? That's my cat. And it's not trapped. I put it there to teach it a lesson."

"We're sure it was our cat," said Mr Fooby-Lartil. "It looked exactly like him."

"I paid a lot of money for that cat," said the Mayor. "I bought it from its owners. They showed me its birth certificate. So it's mine now."

"Perhaps we could just take a look at him," suggested Mrs Fooby-Lartil. "To be sure."

"I told you, it's mine," said the Mayor. "You're not suggesting I stole it, I hope?"

"Certainly not," said Mrs Fooby-Lartil. "But what's the point of having a cat and keeping him in a cell?"

"That cat's special," said the Mayor. "The only one of its kind in the world."

"He looked pretty ordinary to me," said Mr Fooby-Lartil. "Just like ours, in fact. Crooked tail, half an ear missing, that kind of thing."

"It may look ordinary," said the Mayor, "but it's not."

"Really?" said Mr Fooby-Lartil disbelievingly.

The Mayor was annoyed. "I'm telling you it's special," he said. "Unique, in fact. Don't you believe me?"

"It's hard to believe such an ordinary-looking cat could be special," said Mrs Fooby-Lartil.

"He doesn't look much," said Mr Fooby-Lartil. "If it is a he. Is it? Ours is."

The Mayor looked confused. "Of course it's a he," he snapped. "Or a she. One or the other anyway."

"What's his name?" said Mrs Fooby-Lartil.

The Mayor's face went blank.

"Your cat's name," said Mr Fooby-Lartil

kindly.

"It's none of your business," roared the Mayor.

"Funny name for a cat," remarked Mr Fooby-Lartil.

"Go away!" shouted the Mayor. "I'm busy. I can't go wasting time on lost cats."

"I was just wondering," put in Mrs Fooby-Lartil quickly, "why your cat's so special. Can it do tricks or something?"

"Better than that," said the Mayor. He paused. "That cat – my cat – can talk. Speak. The way people do."

Mr Fooby-Lartil gazed at the Mayor. "Well, well," he said sympathetically, like someone humouring a lunatic, "that's very nice. And what does he say?"

"I just told you," said the Mayor. "Everything. He talks like a person. Like you and me."

"I see," said Mr Fooby-Lartil. "And have you had him long?"

"What's that got to do with you?" asked the Mayor.

"Oh, nothing," said Mr Fooby-Lartil. "I was only wondering how many years he's been talking like this."

"You're speaking to me as though I'm crazy," complained the Mayor.

"I never said you were crazy," said Mr Fooby-Lartil. "If you say your cat can talk, no doubt you're absolutely right."

"You don't believe me, do you?" cried the Mayor.

"Talking cats," said Mrs Fooby-Lartil. "I've never seen one, of course, but I'm sure they must exist. It must be possible."

"Funny how you never come across any though," said Mr Fooby-Lartil. "Where did you get him?"

"From two very respectable people," said the Mayor, "who assured me he could say anything, if required."

"What did he say when you bought him?" said Mrs Fooby-Lartil.

"Nothing then," said the Mayor. "They explained he was tired. And nasty-tempered. But they'd heard him talking. They swore it."

"Did you pay them any money for him?" asked Mrs Fooby-Lartil.

"Naturally," said the Mayor. "They weren't going to give him away, were they?" His eyes glistened. "I'll be famous," he said. "Like Dick Whittington. The only mayor in the world with a talking cat. 'Pray stand up for His Worship, the Mayor'."

"If you've paid such a lot for him and he's such a good talker," said Mrs Fooby-Lartil, "why don't you bring him in and prove you haven't wasted your money?"

But as soon as she'd suggested it, she felt worried. What if Percy blurted out something? Or begged them to take him home in front of the Mayor?

"All right then," said the Mayor. "Why not?"

He rang the bell beside him and the Town Clerk came in. He bowed. "Yes, Your Worship?"

"Get that cat and bring it up here right away," said the Mayor.

"Yes, Your Worship," mumbled the Clerk,

walking out backwards and bowing again.

"Now you'll see," said the Mayor. "A talking cat. The only one of its kind in the entire world. Worth every penny I paid for it!"

Chapter 19

A few minutes later, the Town Clerk reappeared with Percy trembling beside him. Mr Fooby-Lartil was furious. Percy looked so thin and frightened. Mrs Fooby-Lartil frowned at her husband. He knew what she was thinking. If he snatched Percy and took him home, the Mayor would have them all arrested and they'd be even worse off. He nodded slightly to show he understood. Percy was gazing at them pleadingly.

"He certainly looks intelligent," said Mrs Fooby-Lartil to the Mayor. Then, staring straight at Percy, she added, "*But I'm absolutely sure he isn't going to talk, no matter what you say*."

Percy understood instantly. He waved his tail a fraction and lowered his eyelids.

"Watch this," said the Mayor. "I'll show you you're wrong. Come here, cat."

Percy stayed where he was.

"Come here," repeated the Mayor.

Percy didn't move.

"Bring him here," said the Mayor to the Town Clerk. The Town Clerk approached Percy gingerly and tried to lift him up. Percy shot out a long needled claw and stuck it into the Town Clerk's arm.

"Yow!" shouted the Clerk. "Ow, yow. Get him off me!"

"Don't be ridiculous," said the Mayor. "It's only a cat."

"With claws like a tiger," said the Town Clerk sulkily. "See. My arm's bleeding. I need a bandage."

The Mayor fished round under his seat, pulled out a first-aid box and handed him a big white bandage.

He turned to Percy. "Say hello," he ordered.

"Miaow," said Percy.

"He—ll—oh," said the Mayor. "Say hello."

"Miaow," said Percy again.

"It doesn't sound like hello," said Mr Fooby-Lartil. "It sounds like miaow to me."

"Of course it's miaow," snapped the Mayor. "He hasn't said hello yet."

"When's he going to?" asked Mrs Fooby-Lartil.

"*I* don't know," said the Mayor irritably. "I didn't train him."

"Who did?" said Mr Fooby-Lartil.

"The Grimbotts, I expect," said the Mayor.

"The *Grimbotts*!" exploded Mr Fooby-Lartil then, catching himself just in time, he added, "How fascinating. Did they tell you how they did it?"

"No need," said the Mayor. "Once he's trained he's trained for good."

"He doesn't seem very trained to me," said Mrs Fooby-Lartil. "He hasn't spoken yet."

The Mayor beckoned to the Town Clerk. "Fetch two saucers of mackerel and cream right away," he said.

"My arm hurts," complained the Town Clerk.

"If you don't do as you're told, your bottom'll be hurting as well," said the Mayor.

The Town Clerk scurried off.

The Fooby-Lartils looked at each other in dismay.

"Percy's going to find that cream and mackerel very hard to resist," thought Mrs Fooby-Lartil.

"Watch," said the Mayor. He laid out the

cream and mackerel saucers and took hold of Percy by the scruff of the neck.

"There," he said. "All yours if you just say, 'You're a kind and wonderful Mayor. Thank you.'"

Percy gazed at the food. A thin dribble of saliva ran down his chin. "Uh, oh," thought Mr Fooby-Lartil. Percy made a move towards the saucers, quivering with anticipation. Then he raised his head, looked at the Fooby-Lartils and stepped back again. He took a deep sniff of the mackerel.

"It seems very cruel," said Mr Fooby-Lartil. "Starving the poor thing and then showing him food he can't have."

"He can have it," said the Mayor. "All he's got to do is talk."

"But what if he can't talk?" said Mrs Fooby-Lartil. "What if the Grimbotts have tricked you?"

"Nobody tricks me," said the Mayor. He shook Percy. "Go on," he said. " 'You're a kind and wonderful Mayor. Thank you.' Say it and the food's yours. And there's plenty more where that came from."

Percy stared desperately at the mackerel, then at the Fooby-Lartils. "Maybe he'd be better off living with the Mayor," thought Mr Fooby-Lartil. "At least he'd get regular meals." Then he noticed again the Mayor's mean little eyes and spiteful expression. "Definitely not," he decided.

"Bring the saucers closer," ordered the Mayor. Percy's nose was only centimetres away from the mackerel now. He looked piteously at the Fooby-Lartils, closed his eyes, opened his mouth and started, "You . . ."

"See," said the Mayor triumphantly. "I told you."

Chapter 20

Mrs Fooby-Lartil looked sadly at her husband. He sighed.

"Poor Percy," he was thinking. "No wonder he couldn't resist."

"You . . . o . . . owwww . . . oowwwwwww . . . owwwlllllll!" shouted Percy, throwing back his head and caterwauling as loudly as he could. "Yow . . . yow . . . hisssssssss." He spat at the Mayor for good measure.

"Get away!" shouted the Mayor, hitting out at Percy. And Mrs Fooby-Lartil decided she'd had enough. "Stop that at once," she cried to the astonished Mayor. "Of course he can't talk. Don't be ridiculous. Whoever heard of a talking cat? The Grimbotts have tricked you. He's our cat and they stole him. And if you've been silly enough to buy him, that's your problem. We're taking him home right now."

And she picked up Percy and tucked him under her arm. Percy nestled against the piglet in her pocket.

"Put that cat down this minute!" bellowed the Mayor. "Or I'll have you arrested!"

"Give him to me," said Mr Fooby-Lartil, taking Percy. "You heard my wife," he said to the Mayor. "We're taking him home."

A tear trickled down Percy's cheek. He leaned against Mr Fooby-Lartil's jacket.

"I'm calling the police!" cried the Mayor. He pressed a button on the arm of his chair and a siren could be heard shrilling in the distance.

"Jail for you," said the Mayor, "and the cat stays with me."

Mrs Fooby-Lartil smiled. "I expect the police will be very amused when they hear how the Grimbotts tricked the Mayor," she remarked.

"He'll be a laughing stock, all right," said Mr Fooby-Lartil. He grinned. "It *is* quite funny," he said. "Fancy anyone imagining a cat could talk."

"People may start wondering whether he's clever enough to *be* the Mayor," went on Mrs Fooby-Lartil.

"What do you mean?" demanded the Mayor. "Nobody tricks me."

"The Grimbotts have," said Mr Fooby-Lartil.

"They have not," said the Mayor.

"Of course they have," said Mrs Fooby-Lartil. "They told you that cat could talk and you believed them."

"You even paid them money for him," pointed out Mr Fooby-Lartil. "And he can't say a word."

"Miaow," said Percy.

"Except miaow," added Mrs Fooby-Lartil. "People will think you're really stupid."

"You're not to tell them," said the Mayor. "I forbid you."

"You can't forbid us," said Mr Fooby-Lartil. "Listen. I think that's the police."

"Sounds like it," said Mrs Fooby-Lartil. "I can't wait to tell them."

"Don't you dare!" bellowed the Mayor.

"I'll do as I like," said Mrs Fooby-Lartil, "and you can't stop me."

There was a loud rapping at the door. "Police," called a gruff voice.

"Wait! Wait!" shouted the Mayor. He

turned to the Fooby-Lartils. "All right," he said angrily. "You win. I'll send them away."

Two large policemen pushed open the door. They bowed.

"Everything all right, Guv?" said one.

"Er, fine," said the Mayor. "I accidentally pushed the panic button, that's all. I won't be needing you."

"Right," said the policeman.

The Mayor waited till their footsteps had died away in the distance, then he glared at the Fooby-Lartils and shook his fist. "Take that blasted cat and get out right now," he hissed.

"And if I find you've said one word to anyone, I'll . . . I'll . . . I'll . . ."

"Yes?" said Mr Fooby-Lartil.

"I'll make you suffer for it," said the Mayor. "And I'll get you for this. Just you wait and see!"

Chapter 21

Percy lay back in Mr Fooby-Lartil's arms. "It's wonderful to be home," he purred.

"Good," said Mr Fooby-Lartil. "It's nice to have you back."

"I've decided," said Percy, "I'll be good. I'll be kind. I won't complain. I'll be a help." He looked down at his saucer. "That's my second-best one," he said. "Why's it out?" He sprang down from Mr Fooby-Lartil's arms. "It's that piglet," he said. "*He's* been using it. *My* saucer! What a cheek! Without even asking."

"You weren't here to ask," pointed out Mr Fooby-Lartil.

"Behind my back," said Percy theatrically.

"While I was locked up and suffering. Stealing my things. I wouldn't be surprised if he asked the Grimbotts to thieve me so he could have my saucer!"

"Stop being ridiculous," said Mr Fooby-Lartil. "You just said you were going to be kind."

"Not to him, I didn't," said Percy. "I've got my limits." He stalked off outside.

"Well, it looks as if Percy's back to normal," said Mr Fooby-Lartil. "I think I'll go and get on with my Teamaker. The tap valve's sticking but I've almost cracked it this time."

Chapter 22

"Come here," said the Mayor to the Town Clerk.

The Town Clerk edged nervously towards him.

"You haven't heard anything about talking cats, you haven't seen any talking cats, you've never seen those wretched Fooby-Lartils and they weren't in the Town Hall. Understand that?" said the Mayor.

"Y . . . yes," said the Town Clerk. "Naturally. Of course. Anything you say."

"I'll deal with the Grimbotts later," said the Mayor. "Nobody gets the better of me. And especially not two stupid inventors and a cat.

I'm going to teach them a lesson that'll make them sorry. I've had an extremely clever idea. And here it is."

He beckoned the Town Clerk closer and whispered in his ear. The Town Clerk smiled. "Very good," he said. "Rather like killing two birds with one stone, Your Worship."

"I'm not Mayor for nothing," said the Mayor proudly. "Now go and get those posters sorted out."

"Right away, Your Worship," said the Town Clerk.

The Mayor lay back in his chair. "That'll teach them," he said to himself. And he smiled a mean, glittery little smile.

Chapter 23

"There's a lot of people looking at notices on the trees in town," announced Percy, coming in with two potatoes and some bacon rinds. "And look what I found at the market."

"Bacon," said Mrs Fooby-Lartil. "My favourite. Thank you, Percy. I'll make some nourishing soup for tonight."

"You didn't by any chance find an onion as well, did you?" said Mr Fooby-Lartil. "That'd make it really tasty."

"Some people," said Percy, "are never satisfied. You carry home two heavy potatoes and all they want is an onion. Huh!"

Mrs Fooby-Lartil frowned at her husband.

"You could go and look yourself after the market's closed," she said. "You never know what you might find. What did the notices say, Percy?"

"I couldn't see," said Percy. "Too many people in the way." He looked at Mrs Fooby-Lartil's pocket. "He's gone!" he cried. "You finally got rid of him. Thank goodness. I thought it smelt fresher in here."

"Percy!" said Mrs Fooby-Lartil. "Stop that at once. Of course I haven't got rid of him. He's stopped being so frightened now. He's over there sleeping in the corner."

"On *my* coat!" shouted Percy. "Thank you very much."

He made a dive for the legwarmer but Mr Fooby-Lartil was too quick for him. He seized Percy by the scruff of the neck and swung him up into the air.

"Ow! Help! Put me down!" shrieked Percy.

"You'd better get this straight once and for all," said Mr Fooby-Lartil. "You are *not*, repeat, not, to terrorise that piglet."

"And it isn't your legwarmer," said Mrs

Fooby-Lartil. "It's the other one."

"I don't want him having the same as me," muttered Percy. "It's not fair. I want to be seen wearing a smart coat, not a pig's bed."

"Put a sock in it, Percy," said Mr Fooby-Lartil.

"Sock, legwarmer. Ha, ha, very funny, I'm sure," said Percy. "And look what he's done to it. He's sucked all the edges and ruined them."

"Why not try being friendly to him?" suggested Mrs Fooby-Lartil.

"He's not my friend," said Percy. "I don't want to be seen trotting round with a piglet. What'll the Grimbotts' cat think?"

"I didn't know you minded what the Grimbotts' cat thought," said Mrs Fooby-Lartil.

"And I shouldn't have thought you'd want to go anywhere near the Grimbotts' after what happened," said Mr Fooby-Lartil.

"I don't go near the Grimbotts' place," said Percy haughtily. "She drops in on me occasionally, that's all. In fact, she's probably waiting for me now."

He headed off outside, then paused in the doorway. "And make sure that piglet doesn't make a mistake," he said darkly. "If I get back and find it's been sleeping on *my* legwarmer . . ." He slammed the door behind him.

"Being in the cells hasn't improved his manners," said Mrs Fooby-Lartil.

"Just the opposite," said Mr Fooby-Lartil. "I think I'll go and hunt for that onion now. See you later. 'Bye."

Mrs Fooby-Lartil put the kettle on for a cup of boiling water.

"Thank goodness you can't talk," she said to the piglet. "Peace and quiet at last."

Chapter 24

Mr Fooby-Lartil burst through the door, clutching a piece of paper and a large onion.

"Good," said Mrs Fooby-Lartil. "I can easily cut out the squashed bits."

Mr Fooby-Lartil waved the paper impatiently. "Forget the onion!" he cried. "This is what counts. Look, look. Read it. Quick!"

"If you let go of it for a minute, I'll be able to," said Mrs Fooby-Lartil.

"There," said Mr Fooby-Lartil, stabbing the paper with his finger.

"Where?" said Percy.

"Stop it or I'll never see what it says," said Mrs Fooby-Lartil. She smoothed out the paper and laid it on the table.

☆ **GRAND MYSTERY PRIZE** ☆

THE MAYOR IS OFFERING A BAG OF GOLD COINS

AND

A GRAND MYSTERY PRIZE

TO THE WINNER OF THIS COMPETITION

☆

DESIGN A SENSIBLE, ORIGINAL, FIRST CLASS
INVENTION

SUITABLE FOR THE MAYOR TO USE
TO IMPROVE HIS TOWN HALL
AND SHOW HIS IMPORTANCE
ALL OVER THE WORLD

☆

COMPETITION CLOSES AT SUNDOWN TOMORROW
AND
THE PRIZE WILL BE AWARDED
A WEEK BEFORE CHRISTMAS

Maximum two entries per competitor

she read.

"Well," said Mr Fooby-Lartil, "what do you think?"

"Wonderful," said Mrs Fooby-Lartil. "Just made for us."

"You're bound to win," said Percy excitedly. He turned to Mrs Fooby-Lartil. "What about those shampoo pads for the paws I ment . . ."

"We've only got till sundown tomorrow," said Mrs Fooby-Lartil. "We'll have to enter something that's already finished. Or nearly complete. We haven't got much time."

"I'll do the cooking," said Percy. "You two start work straight away."

Chapter 25

"I've got the Self-Making Bed ready," said Mrs Fooby-Lartil. "That might win."

"What about your Flattering-Footwiper?" said Mr Fooby-Lartil. "The Mayor'd like that."

"Yes," said Mrs Fooby-Lartil. "All it needs is a few adjustments. I'll bring it down and try it out. What are you going to enter?"

"My Teamaker," said Mr Fooby-Lartil.

"I wouldn't give that Teamaker a prize," said Percy.

"It's not you who's giving the Grand Mystery Prize," said Mr Fooby-Lartil. "It's the Mayor."

"I'd rather have the coins than the Grand Mystery Prize," said Percy. "At least you know what you're getting."

"You get both," pointed out Mrs Fooby-Lartil. She sighed. "Just imagine if we won. We'd never have to worry about money again."

"You won't win if you don't start soon," said Percy. "Get a move on."

"You're right," said Mrs Fooby-Lartil. "I'll go and get the Footwiper now."

She came back downstairs carrying a brown hairy mat.

"That's not very promising," said Percy. "It isn't going to win on appearance."

"Nor would you," said Mr Fooby-Lartil.

Percy looked hurt.

"Stop it at once," said Mrs Fooby-Lartil. "Both of you."

"Sorry," said Mr Fooby-Lartil.

"Would you mind trying the Footwiper, Percy?" said Mrs Fooby-Lartil.

"What does it do?" asked Percy

apprehensively.

"You stand on it and it wipes your feet for you," explained Mrs Fooby-Lartil. "And all the while it tells you how wonderful you are."

"The Mayor'll love that," said Percy. "Do I have to switch it on?"

"No," said Mrs Fooby-Lartil. "Just stand on it."

Percy stood gingerly on the brown mat. Immediately it began to move backwards and forwards, forwards and back. "Ow!" shrieked Percy. "It's hurting me. It's taking the soles off my paws. Yow! Stop it."

"Jump off," said Mrs Fooby-Lartil. "That'll stop it."

Percy limped over to Mr Fooby-Lartil's favourite chair and sat in it.

"I'm terribly sorry," said Mrs Fooby-Lartil. "I forgot you need to be wearing shoes."

"Ruined," moaned Percy. "Destroyed. I may never walk again."

"It's not that bad," said Mr Fooby-Lartil. "It's only coir matting."

"It felt more like barbed wire," said Percy faintly.

"Shall I rub your paws?" asked Mrs Fooby-Lartil.

"No," said Percy. "Leave them alone. I don't think I could stand to have anyone touch them right now."

Mr Fooby-Lartil stood on the Footwiper. "Try me," he said. Immediately the Footwiper began to move and a metallic voice could be heard from inside the matting. "You're tremendous," it said. "You're wonderful. You're stupendous. It's an honour to be allowed to wipe the mud from your filthy shoes."

"Yuk," said Percy. "Listen to it." He turned to Mrs Fooby-Lartil. "Don't let *him* use it," he said. "He's bad enough already."

"The piglet's lying on your legwarmer," said Mr Fooby-Lartil.

Percy leapt to his paws. "Where?" he demanded. "Spoilt brat. I'll show him."

"I see your paws have improved," said Mr Fooby-Lartil.

Percy turned angrily towards him and spat. "One of these days . . ." he said as he limped ostentatiously back to Mr Fooby-Lartil's chair.

"Percy," said Mrs Fooby-Lartil, "I need your opinion. Do you think the Mayor might choose this invention?"

Percy thought for a minute. "Yes," he said. "He'll really love it. You should definitely enter that one." He glowered at Mr Fooby-Lartil. "I certainly hope you win," he said to Mrs Fooby-Lartil. "Unlike others I could mention."

"Thank you," said Mrs Fooby-Lartil.

"Pleasure," said Percy. "Better than that stupid Teamaker any day!"

Chapter 26

"So it's my Footwiper, my Bed and your Teamaker," said Mrs Fooby-Lartil. "Are you sure the Teamaker's all right?"

"Perfect," said Mr Fooby-Lartil. "I've totally cracked it now."

"A cracked teamaker," said Percy. "Doesn't sound too good to me."

"Put a sock in it, Percy," said Mr Fooby-Lartil irritably. He turned to Mrs Fooby-Lartil. "Only one problem now. How do we get the Bed to the Town Hall?"

"Easy," said Mrs Fooby-Lartil. "It can walk. It's got feet."

"It doesn't want to go," said Percy from the

depths of Mr Fooby-Lartil's chair. "I saw it crying. It doesn't want to live with the Mayor."

"Oh dear," said Mrs Fooby-Lartil.

"Don't be silly," said Mr Fooby-Lartil. "I'll go and get it now."

He came back with the Bed clattering behind him. Great tears welled out of the slits in its feet and ran across the floor.

"Maybe I shouldn't enter it," said Mrs Fooby-Lartil.

"You're too soft-hearted," said Mr Fooby-Lartil. "It's only a bed."

"I suppose so," said Mrs Fooby-Lartil.

Mr Fooby-Lartil picked up his Troublefree-Teamaker and the Footwiper with the notice attached—FLATTERING-FOOTWIPER: MRS FOOBY-LARTIL—and they set off with the Bed sniffling beside them.

"Bye," said Percy from the chair.

"I suppose," said Mr Fooby-Lartil, "that it's too much to expect you to have dinner on the table when we get back."

"Dead right," said Percy, waving his paws in the air. "Much too much. Remember, I'm injured."

"I'm having trouble forgetting it," muttered Mr Fooby-Lartil, shutting the door behind them.

chapter 27

"Look at all these inventions," said the Mayor. "Fantastic, isn't it?"

"An awful lot of people seem to have entered," said the Town Clerk. "I didn't know that was what you wanted."

"See this," said the Mayor. He put on a tiara with a band of coloured lights at the front. "When I press this switch it lights up so everyone can read it."

"THE MAYOR IS FANTASTIC" flashed the lights. The Mayor pressed another switch. "WHAT A MARVELLOUS MAYOR" spelt the lights.

"I think this one should win," said the

THE MAYOR IS FANTASTIC

Mayor. "Just what I need."

"But," said the Clerk, "you said the Fooby-Lartils had to win."

The Mayor sighed. "Pity," he said. "But you're right. I did say that. Let's give her Bed first prize, her Footwiper second prize and his Teamaker third prize. Actually," he went on, "I quite like the Footwiper. Got the right idea. Seems to rather admire me."

The Town Clerk grunted to himself. Then he said, "You do realise this means parting with a bag of gold coins, a bag of silver coins *and* a certificate."

"But think of what I'm saving in the long run," said the Mayor. "Worth it. Definitely worth it."

Chapter 28

A large crowd had collected in the town square by the time the Fooby-Lartils and Percy arrived. Mrs Fooby-Lartil was trembling with excitement. "Suppose we've won," she whispered.

"We won't have," said Percy gloomily, taking in the huge crowd. "Too much competition."

"Someone's got to win," said Mrs Fooby-Lartil. "Why not us?"

"Ssh," said Mr Fooby-Lartil. "Here comes the Town Clerk."

The Town Clerk climbed on to the podium. "I am ordered by our world-famous Mayor," he said, "to announce the winners of the Grand Mystery Prize Competition. His Worship the Mayor has come to a decision. A difficult decision in view of the number and uniformly high standard of design of the entries."

"Someone's designed a uniform," hissed Percy. "And we've lost. I knew we would."

"Sssh," whispered Mrs Fooby-Lartil.

"The third prize of a framed certificate signed personally by the Mayor," announced the Town Clerk, "goes to Mr Fooby-Lartil for his Totally-Troublefree-Time-Tested-Teamaker."

"Hurray!" shouted the crowd.

Mr Fooby-Lartil looked disappointed.

"A certificate," said Percy. "Signed by the Mayor. Yuk!"

"And the second prize of a bag of silver coins," went on the Town Clerk, "goes to Mrs Fooby-Lartil for her Flattering Footwiper."

Most people clapped, though one or two were heard muttering, "Fix," and "Rigged."

Mr Fooby-Lartil patted his wife warmly on

the back. "Wonderful," he said. "Clever you!"

"Silver coins," said Mrs Fooby-Lartil. "We'll never be hungry again." But secretly she couldn't help wishing it had been the Grand Mystery Prize.

She and Mr Fooby-Lartil had spent all evening wondering what it might be. She was certain it was a holiday or perhaps even a special inventing shed. But Mr Fooby-Lartil was sure it was a car. The Fooby-Lartils had always wanted a car. She shook herself. She was being silly. A bag of silver coins was wonderful. She smiled at Mr Fooby-Lartil.

"Go on," he said. "Go up and collect your prize."

And as she was walking back with the bag of coins, Mrs Fooby-Lartil heard the Town Clerk announcing the winner of the Grand Mystery Prize.

"The Grand Mystery Prize and the bag of gold coins," he said importantly, "have been won by . . ." He paused. Mrs Fooby Lartil looked around her. Who was going to be the lucky winner?

"Mrs Fooby-Lartil," said the Town Clerk. "For her Self-Making Bed."

Mrs Fooby-Lartil felt her legs go rubbery with excitement. Hands were pushing her towards the podium again.

The Town Clerk handed her a heavy bag of gold coins.

Mrs Fooby-Lartil could hardly believe it. They'd misjudged the Mayor. He hadn't been too upset by what had happened with Percy, after all. He'd even awarded them not just one but *all* of the prizes. She smiled at the Town Clerk. "What is the Grand Mystery Prize?" she asked.

"Tomorrow night," said the Clerk, "the Mayor himself will present the Grand Mystery Prize at the Town Hall at six o'clock sharp."

"Cheat!" called a voice from the back of the crowd.

"Unfair!" shouted someone else.

"Quiet, please!" cried the Town Clerk. "The Mayor's decision is final. Three cheers for Mrs Fooby-Lartil."

"Hurrah!" shouted most of the crowd.

"Hurrah! Hurrah!"

And Mrs Fooby-Lartil thought she'd never felt happier in her life.

Chapter 29

"Brilliant. Superb," said Percy on the way home. "I said all along you'd win the lot."

Mrs Fooby-Lartil swung the gold coins as she walked. "I can't wait to see the Grand Mystery Prize tomorrow," she said.

"Me too," said Mr Fooby-Lartil, swinging the silver coins to and fro.

"Maybe it *is* a car," said Mrs Fooby-Lartil.

And just as she spoke, she tripped on a stone and fell, wrenching her ankle.

"I can't move," she said miserably. "I think I've sprained it."

"Percy and I'll carry you home," said Mr Fooby-Lartil. "I'll tie both lots of coins round

my belt."

"You'll have to pick up the Grand Mystery Prize for me tomorrow, I'm afraid," said Mrs Fooby-Lartil. "I won't be able to walk on this foot for a few days."

"No problem," said Mr Fooby-Lartil. "Percy and I'll collect it together and bring it home and surprise you. Now I think all this success calls for a celebration, don't you, Percy?"

"Definitely," said Percy. "Make mine cream and mackerel if you don't mind."

Chapter 30

"I do wish I could go," said Mrs Fooby-Lartil next day, "but my ankle still collapses if I stand on it."

"Don't worry," said Mr Fooby-Lartil. "Percy and I'll get it and bring it straight home. Won't we, Percy?"

Percy nodded.

"I was thinking," said Mrs Fooby-Lartil, "it might be a holiday. I can't help hoping. We've never had a holiday. Maybe it's a trip to the seaside."

"Or it could be a new house," said Mr Fooby-Lartil.

"That's a bit grand," said Mrs Fooby-Lartil.

"It says 'Grand' on the notices," said Mr Fooby-Lartil.

"I know what I think it is," said Percy. "A pond full of mackerel. But I'm sick of standing round waiting. It's nearly six o'clock. If we go and get it, we'll know what it is instead of guessing."

"Sensible," said Mrs Fooby-Lartil. "But please come back with it right away. I'm longing to see what it is."

"We'll be back the instant we've got it," promised Mr Fooby-Lartil. "You know, this is definitely the most amazing thing that's ever happened to us."

Chapter 31

Mr Fooby-Lartil came slowly up the path. "I'm not telling her," said Percy from behind him. "You took the prize. You brought it home. Now you tell her."

"Put a sock in it, Percy," said Mr Fooby-Lartil. He could hear Mrs Fooby-Lartil whistling in the kitchen. He peeped in through the window. She was wearing her best green and red spotted inventor coat with a big flowery hat . . . and on the table . . . Mr Fooby-Lartil's heart thumped: his mouth dribbled. "Look at that," he whispered to Percy. Percy hauled himself up by the front legs and gazed in.

The table was set with jellies, ice-cream, crisps, baby sausages, chicken, special chocolate raspberry biscuits, cream cakes, chocolate éclairs and a great big yellow iced cake with

CLEVER US
WE WON

picked out in purple icing.

"Yum!" shouted Mr Fooby-Lartil, racing in through the door, snatching an éclair and cramming it into his mouth.

Percy slunk in behind him. "Now the real trouble starts," he muttered, licking up some cream that had fallen to the floor.

"Eat it up! Enjoy it!" cried Mrs Fooby-Lartil. "It's a special, stupendous celebration. I sent Percy to the baker's this afternoon." She clutched her husband's arm. "Have another éclair," she said excitedly, "and then tell me where the Grand Mystery Prize is. You did get it, didn't you?"

"Oh yes," said Mr Fooby-Lartil. "We got it all right. Didn't we Percy?"

Percy was busily washing himself.

"It's outside," said Mr Fooby-Lartil. "In the garden. Isn't it, Percy?"

Percy went on washing.

"I thought it might be a new house with two inventing sheds," said Mrs Fooby-Lartil, "but if you've got it in the garden, it can't be that."

"No," said Mr Fooby-Lartil, "it's not that."

Mrs Fooby-Lartil hugged him. "Just imagine," she said, "we've finally done it. We've won a big prize at last."

"It was you who won it," said Mr Fooby-Lartil.

"Yes, but we always share everything," said Mrs Fooby-Lartil, "so you must have half."

Percy gave a loud cough.

"And Percy too, of course," said Mrs Fooby-Lartil.

"It's all right, thanks," said Percy. "It's your prize. I don't mind going without."

Mr Fooby-Lartil said nothing.

"You know," said Mrs Fooby-Lartil, through a mouthful of jelly and ice-cream, "I wasn't even sure there *would* be a prize. The Mayor's so mean, I thought he'd try to get out of awarding one somehow. It shows you: there's good in everybody." She took another sausage roll.

Mr Fooby-Lartil looked uneasily at Percy.

"About the prize . . ." he began.

"No, don't tell me," said Mrs Fooby-Lartil. "I want it to be a surprise."

"I think I should tell you," said Mr Fooby-Lartil nervously.

Mrs Fooby-Lartil looked anxious. "There *is* a prize, isn't there?" she said.

"Yes, yes," said Mr Fooby-Lartil. "There's definitely a prize and you've definitely won it. But it's not a very usual sort of prize."

Mrs Fooby-Lartil smiled. "I don't mind," she said. "I told you, I love surprises. Let's go and see what it is."

Mr Fooby-Lartil didn't move.

"Come on," said his wife, pulling at his sleeve.

"Percy'll show you," said Mr Fooby-Lartil desperately.

"Oh, no, he won't," said Percy. He pointed an accusing paw at Mr Fooby-Lartil. "You got

181

us into this. Now you get us out of it."

Mrs Fooby-Lartil looked bewildered. "I don't understand," she said. "Why can't you show me the Grand Mystery Prize and have done with it?"

"I'm off," said Percy, going outside.

"I want to see the Grand Mystery Prize," said Mrs Fooby-Lartil in ominous tones, "*right this minute*."

Mr Fooby-Lartil got up from his chair. "All right," he said unhappily. "If you're sure."

Suddenly from the garden there came a loud wail, then another, and another and another and another . . . and another . . . and another . . .

"What on earth's that?" said Mrs Fooby-Lartil.

Percy burst back inside. "This is it!" he shouted. "The final straw! A nursemaid, that's all I am. Nothing but a nursemaid. One of you two can come and sort it out. You won them, you come and look after them. I've a good mind to leave home right this minute."

"Tell me what's going on," cried Mrs

Fooby-Lartil.

Mr Fooby-Lartil took a deep breath. "It's the Grand Mystery Prize," he said. "Seventeen babies. I'm sorry, I really am, but that's what you've won."

Chapter 32

"SEVENTEEN BABIES!!" shrieked Mrs Fooby-Lartil. "Don't be ridiculous!"

She raced outside. Sitting on the path was an enormous pram. From inside came screams and howls.

"Where did they come from?" she demanded.

"The Mayor," said Mr Fooby-Lartil.

"I know that," said Mrs Fooby-Lartil, exasperated. "But where did he get them? They can't have just come out of nowhere."

"They were left over after a baby show," explained Mr Fooby-Lartil. "The whole competition was a set-up by the Mayor. He

wanted to get back at us for Percy *and* get rid of
the babies at the same time."

"Well, we're not keeping them," said Mrs
Fooby-Lartil. "And that's final." She peered
into the pram. "But I suppose they'd be quite
sweet really, if they weren't all crying."

"Quite hideous, if you ask me," said Percy,
coming up behind them.

"We didn't," said Mr Fooby-Lartil.

"And *very* hungry," continued Percy. "You'd better give them something to eat. Lucky they don't like sardines and mackerel."

"We're not giving them anything to eat," said Mrs Fooby-Lartil firmly. "You're taking them right back to the Mayor now, this minute."

"Not me," said Percy. "I didn't accept them. He did."

Mr Fooby-Lartil sighed. "All right, all right," he said. He seized the pram handle and gave it a shove. "It's too heavy. You'll have to help me push it, Percy."

"I've got a sore paw," said Percy. "Not that anyone round here cares."

"Please," said Mr Fooby-Lartil. "The sooner we get them back, the sooner our troubles are over."

"I wouldn't count on it," said Percy grimly. "That's the Town Clerk coming in the gate and he doesn't look too happy to me."

The Town Clerk marched up the path. "The Mayor wants to see you immediately," he said. "And you're in big trouble this time."

Chapter 33

By the time they reached the Town Hall everyone was in a temper. The babies were cross because they were hungry, Percy was cross because his paw hurt, Mr Fooby-Lartil was cross because his back hurt, Mrs Fooby-Lartil was cross because her ankle hurt and the Town Clerk was very cross indeed because he'd had to give Mrs Fooby-Lartil a piggy-back all the way.

But when they got inside, they found the Mayor was even more furious than any of them.

"What do you *mean* by it?" he shouted. "How *dare* you insult me? I'm calling the police. It's outrageous!"

"He's still got his pyjamas on," whispered Percy. "And it's teatime."

"And they're pink," hissed Mr Fooby-Lartil.

"With a hole in the bottom," said Mrs Fooby-Lartil.

"Shut up!" bellowed the Mayor. "And keep those babies quiet while I'm talking!"

"They're your babies," said Mrs Fooby-Lartil. "We're giving them back. So you can keep them quiet yourself."

"You can't give them back," said the Mayor. "You won them. *I* don't want them. I can't afford to feed them." He glared at the Fooby-Lartils. "Just come upstairs and see what you've done," he said.

The Town Clerk sighed deeply as he hitched Mrs Fooby-Lartil onto his back again. "Forty-two stairs," he complained.

"Stop that griping," said the Mayor. "Or you're out of a job." He threw open his bedroom door. "Look!"

The Bed was standing forlornly in the

middle of the room.

"What's wrong with it?" said Mrs Fooby-Lartil.

"This," said the Mayor. He pulled down the sheet. "It's apple-pied itself. That bed was perfectly normal when I went to sleep last night and this morning I couldn't get out of the sheets." He pointed to the Town Clerk. "He had to pull me free. Now fix it at once."

Very slowly, the Bed raised its foot and landed a hard kick on the Mayor's shin.

"Ow!" he shrieked. "Help."

Mrs Fooby-Lartil glared at the Mayor over the Town Clerk's shoulder. "There's nothing wrong with it," she said, "so I can't fix it. It doesn't like you, that's all. And no wonder. Wearing pink pyjamas at your age. It's disgusting."

"She's right," said Mr Fooby-Lartil. "The Bed comes home with us and you can keep the Grand Mystery Prize."

Percy plucked at Mr Fooby-Lartil's sleeve and rolled his eyes. "What do you want?" said Mr Fooby-Lartil.

Percy rolled his eyes again.

"Excuse me," said Mr Fooby-Lartil, scooping up Percy and leaving the bedroom.

"Come back here!" shouted the Mayor.

"When we're ready," called Mr Fooby-Lartil.

"All right, Percy," he whispered. "What is it?"

Percy looked embarrassed. "They're hideous, of course," he said. "And noisy, too. But they don't like sardines or mackerel, so that's all right . . ."

"What are you talking about?" demanded Mr Fooby-Lartil.

"The babies," said Percy. "We can't leave them with *him*. He won't be kind to them."

Mr Fooby-Lartil nodded. "You're right," he said. "Of course we can't and we don't know who owns them so we'll have to keep them."

"That's what I think," said Percy.

"But you'll have to help," said Mr Fooby-Lartil.

Percy sighed. "All right," he said. "But I'm

not pushing the pram. And that's definite."

"We'll go and tell the Mayor," said Mr Fooby-Lartil. "And we'll take Mrs Fooby-Lartil home in the Bed. Much more comfortable than the Town Clerk's knobbly back."

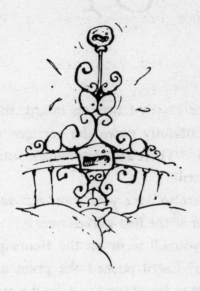

Chapter 34

With Mrs Fooby-Lartil on board, the Bed stepped carefully down the corridor to the front door. "There's the Footwiper," said Mrs Fooby-Lartil.

"Pleasure to wipe your tootsies," said the Footwiper as the Bed walked over it.

"And yours," went on the Footwiper as Mr Fooby-Lartil pushed the pram across. "It's a joy to be allowed to take the mud off your shoes. You're wonderful, you're marvellous . . ."

"All right, all right," said Mr Fooby-Lartil, watching as Percy leapt the Footwiper. "Put a sock in it."

The Mayor stood on the Footwiper, shaking his fist as they left. "Good riddance!" he shouted.

"Delighted to have you rub your filthy feet on me," cooed the Footwiper. Then suddenly its tone changed. "Careful," it snapped."Mind your big feet, you clumsy oaf."

"Don't speak to me like that," said the Mayor, kicking at it.

"Your feet smell," said the Footwiper. "You should wash them more often."

"I'll throw you out with the garbage," threatened the Mayor.

The Footwiper swayed to and fro and shook itself several times, then as the Fooby-Lartils and Percy watched, it slowly . . .

rose . . .

and rose . . .

and rose . . .

until . . .

it changed into a porcupine and crawled away
down the steps.

"Time we were off," said Mrs Fooby-Lartil.

Chapter 35

"We'll have to feed the babies quickly," said Mrs Fooby-Lartil. "If they scream much longer, I'll go mad."

"Blackberries," said Percy. "That's what they like."

The Fooby-Lartils laughed. "Not yet," said Mr Fooby-Lartil.

"Right now," explained Mrs Fooby-Lartil, "they like milk and mashed banana and . . ."

"*Milk*!!!" shrieked Percy. "Why didn't you tell me?"

"You never asked," said Mr Fooby-Lartil.

"They're not having mine," said Percy, clutching his saucer with both front paws. "I

don't care how hungry they are."

"They don't need yours," said Mrs Fooby-Lartil. "Now we've got the coins, there's plenty for everyone."

"Hhhnnn," said Percy suspiciously.

"I'm a bit disappointed in you, Percy," said Mr Fooby-Lartil. "You're not very generous."

"I'm very, very generous," said Percy, "as long as people don't want *my* things."

"Stop arguing," said Mrs Fooby-Lartil. "The babies need feeding."

"Right," said Mr Fooby-Lartil. "Here, Percy. Take this and nip down and buy seventeen feeding bottles at the chemists'."

He handed Percy a silver coin.

"Me?" said Percy indignantly. "Buying babies' bottles. Not likely."

"Put a sock in it, Percy," said Mr Fooby-Lartil. "You told me to bring them home. On your way *now*! And hurry. This noise is awful."

"They can lie on the Bed with me," said Mrs Fooby-Lartil, "while you warm their milk. Percy won't be long."

"He'd better not be," said Mr Fooby-Lartil. "My ears are hurting."

He was lifting the babies onto the Bed when a thought struck him. "How will we tell which one's which?" he said. "We don't know their names."

"We can call them One, Two, Three . . ." said Mrs Fooby-Lartil.

"Of course we can't," said Mr Fooby-Lartil. "Don't be silly."

The babies lay on the Bed bellowing. "I'll go and heat the milk," said Mr Fooby-Lartil.

"I hope Percy's quick," said Mrs Fooby-Lartil.

The Bed lifted one foot, then the other.

"Oh dear," said Mrs Fooby-Lartil, "now the Bed's going funny."

The Bed stretched out all four arms, wrapped them round the babies, then began to rock from side to side until, one after another, they stopped crying and fell asleep.

Percy pushed open the kitchen door with his tail and staggered in clutching the bottles. "Here you are," he said to Mr Fooby-Lartil, who was stirring a large pan on the stove. "There's a fair on the Common. Can we go?"

"Thanks," said Mr Fooby-Lartil. "Not today. Quick. Help me fill the bottles."

"Listen," said Percy. "The babies've stopped crying."

He peeped round the door. There on the Bed lay the babies and Mrs Fooby-Lartil, all fast asleep.

Chapter 36

"Been up all night," said Mr Fooby-Lartil next morning.

"Inventing what?" said Percy, through a mouthful of sardines on toast.

"This," said Mr Fooby-Lartil grandly.

"Looks like a lot of old elastic and straps on wooden stands," said Percy. "Where's Mrs Fooby-Lartil?"

"Asleep again," said Mr Fooby-Lartil. "She was up half the night with the babies. So I invented this. See."

He set up the stands and rested the funnel on the kitchen table. "Imagine the table's the Bed," he said. "You put a baby on this bit here, pull that switch and the belt goes round like this and then a bottle comes out from there into the baby's mouth and feeds it. It's my new Baby-Management-Conveyor-Belt."

"What about the other end?" said Percy.

"There isn't another end," said Mr Fooby-Lartil. "It's a circle."

"I mean the other end of the baby," said Percy. "The pongy bit. You'll have to do something about that. And don't ask me to . . ."

"I'm not," said Mr Fooby-Lartil. "This bit here does that. It's a nappy-changer and bottom-washer all in one."

"And then the funnel shoots them into the Bed which rocks them to sleep," said Percy. "Clever."

"Thanks," said Mr Fooby-Lartil. "By the way, Mrs Fooby-Lartil says they'll have to have a walk today. Her ankle's almost better but she can't use it till tomorrow. So I wondered . . ."

"Whether Percy could help push them," said Percy. "Humph."

"Just this once," said Mr Fooby-Lartil.

"Just this once," said Percy. "And no more."

"I'll get the babies now," said Mr Fooby-Lartil.

"They're too big for the pram," said Percy as he and Mr Fooby-Lartil pushed it along the lane. "Look at them. They're sticking out everywhere."

"They are a bit squashed," agreed Mr Fooby-Lartil.

"We look ridiculous," said Percy. "Why can't we drive them round in a sports car? Something smart. I've got my self-respect to consider."

"They won't get much fresh air that way," said Mr Fooby-Lartil. "Besides, you can't drive. And nor can I."

"If I had a sports car, I'd learn," said Percy. "Anyway, you're going to have to do something about this pram."

Chapter 37

"The babies are so sweet and friendly," said Mrs Fooby-Lartil, "but they do need entertaining all the time."

"Sweet and friendly!" spluttered Percy. "They keep pulling my tail and ears."

"They don't realise," said Mrs Fooby-Lartil.

"If they had tails," said Percy, "they'd realise."

Mr Fooby-Lartil came in, waving a drawing. "Here it is," he said. "The New-Extended-Multi-Baby-Buggy."

"Before we look at it," said Mrs Fooby-Lartil, "we must do something about their names."

"Naughty . . . Naughtier . . . Even Naughtier
. . . Naughtiest," said Percy feelingly.

"I thought First, Second, Third . . ." said
Mrs Fooby-Lartil.

"No, no," said Mr Fooby-Lartil. "Useless.
They've got to have proper names."

He thought for a while. Then, "I've got it,"
he said, "we'll use the alphabet."

"What's the alphabet?" said Percy.

"The ABC," explained Mr Fooby-Lartil.

"Why not say so then?" said Percy. "Why
call it such a hard name?"

"I don't see what you mean by the ABC,"
said Mrs Fooby-Lartil.

"Booby Fooby-Lartil," said Mr Fooby-
Lartil. "Cooby Fooby-Lartil. Dooby Fooby-
Lartil. Gooby Fooby-Lartil."

"What about Aooby?" said Percy.

"It only works with consonants, not
vowels," said Mr Fooby-Lartil. "B, C, D, G,
H, J . . . that kind of thing."

"I see," said Percy, who didn't.

"Right down to Zooby," said Mr Fooby-

Lartil, pointing to the littlest baby.

"That's the one," said Percy, "that pulls my tail hardest of all."

"We could sew their initials on their clothes so we don't get them muddled up," said Mrs Fooby-Lartil.

"Seventeen of them," said Mr Fooby-Lartil. "That's Booby, Cooby, Dooby, Gooby, Hooby, Jooby . . ."

"Then Looby, Mooby, Nooby and Pooby," said Mrs Fooby-Lartil.

"How many's that?"

"Ten," said Mr Fooby-Lartil. "Then Quooby, Rooby, Sooby, Tooby, Vooby, Wooby, and Zooby. That's seventeen. But Sooby should be Shooby. Otherwise it's too much like Zooby."

"Right," said Mrs Fooby-Lartil. "So they've all got names. Much better. Now what was that drawing you wanted to show me?"

"The buggy," said Mr Fooby-Lartil. "Here." He held it out.

"What happens when you try to go round corners?" said Percy.

"Problems," said Mrs Fooby-Lartil, pulling out her sketch pad. "I've got a better idea. Look."

Percy and Mr Fooby-Lartil peered at her design.

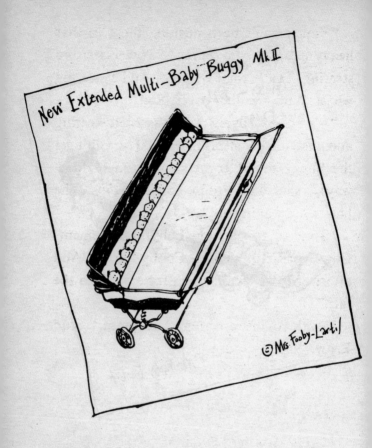

New Extended Multi-Baby Buggy Mk II

© Mrs. Fooby-Lartil

"Wonderful," said Mr Fooby-Lartil.

"Useless," said Percy. "How's it going to get through doorways?"

Mrs Fooby-Lartil looked glum. "I never thought of that," she said.

"You haven't been pushing them in that heavy pram," said Percy. "Power-assisted steering. That's what we need. And a steering wheel. With a leather cover. Red."

"It's no use having power-assisted steering and a red leather steering wheel if we can't get the buggy round corners or through doorways," said Mrs Fooby-Lartil. "Oops. The babies are waking up."

"Time to try out my Baby-Management-Conveyor-Belt," said Mr Fooby-Lartil. "And afterwards we'll take them for a walk to the fair."

"And you're pushing that pram," said Percy. "It's your turn."

Chapter 38

"It's Christmas in three days," said Percy as they walked to the fair. "If I had some money, I could buy presents for certain people."

"Sorry, I quite forgot," said Mr Fooby-Lartil. "Here. Take these."

He handed over some gold and silver coins.

"Thanks," said Percy. "Quite a lot to get this year with all the babies." He glared at Mrs Fooby-Lartil's pocket. "Though some people," he went on, "needn't expect anything from me."

"Would you like to go into the Haunted House?" said Mrs Fooby-Lartil.

"Not me," said Percy. "No *thank* you. You

can go in. I'll just stand there with the pram. Not that I'm frightened or anything," he added hastily.

The Fooby-Lartils jumped aboard the ghost train and vanished.

They came back to find Percy propped against the pram handle staring at the Big Wheel. "Just the thing," he was muttering. "The very thing."

"What?" said Mr Fooby-Lartil.

"The Big Wheel," said Percy. "That's how we should design the baby buggy."

"Brilliant!" cried Mrs Fooby-Lartil. "Excellent. I'll start on it the minute I get home."

Percy beamed. "I told you I was good at inventing," he said proudly. "Now I'll be off to get my Christmas presents."

"The Big Wheel? What on earth does he mean?" said Mr Fooby-Lartil.

"I'll show you when we get home," said Mrs Fooby-Lartil. "And if I'm quick, I might even be able to build it in time for Christmas."

Chapter 39

"Seventeen, eighteen, nineteen, twenty," said Percy, hanging stockings over the fireplace. He paused and looked at the piglet. "I suppose *he'll* have to have one too," he said grudgingly. "Little pest." He nailed up a tiny sock beside the stockings. "Twenty and a half."

"That's Zooby's sock," said Mrs Fooby-Lartil. "I wish you wouldn't make holes in it, Percy."

"Too late now," said Percy. "Maybe Father Christmas won't give him anything anyway." The piglet gave a squeal of dismay.

"If he brings you something, he'll certainly bring him something," said Mrs Fooby-Lartil.

"Now be nice, please. It's Christmas."

"He doesn't make me feel nice . . ." began Percy.

"Bedtime," said Mrs Fooby-Lartil. "Right away. The babies have been asleep for ages and they're sure to wake up early in the morning."

But it was Percy who woke them. "He's been!" he shouted from the stairs. "He's left us all presents in the stockings. Quick! Quick! Come down and see."

"What time is it?" said Mr Fooby-Lartil.

"Four o'clock," said Mrs Fooby-Lartil as the cuckoo clock struck twenty-five. "Go back to sleep, Percy."

Percy appeared in the doorway. "A dummy for each of the babies, a bow for that stupid piglet's tail. And look what I got," he said.

"Go to *sleep*," groaned Mr Fooby-Lartil. "It's the middle of the night."

"A brand new coat," said Percy. "See. Perfect. Really smart and warm. Not a horrible old pig's bed. No. A special one made just for me. And a hat to match. And you've got presents too."

"Percy," said Mr Fooby-Lartil, "get back to bed this minute or you can feed the babies single-handed."

"I'm going," said Percy. "Now." He paused at the top of the stairs. "I just thought you'd like to know," he said in an injured voice.

"Single-handed," said Mr Fooby-Lartil.

"I'm on my way," said Percy, disappearing.

"Sometimes," said Mr Fooby-Lartil, "I wish I'd left Percy in the duckpond."

Chapter 40

After the crackers had been pulled, the Fooby-Lartils and Percy and the piglet and the babies went for a walk.

"To try out the new buggy," said Mrs Fooby-Lartil who had finished it just in time.

"They like it," said Mr Fooby-Lartil. "Especially when they get to the top."

"It fits through doorways," said Percy.

"And round corners," said Mrs Fooby-Lartil.

"A very good idea of mine," said Percy. "Now about those shampoo pads for the paws that I was ment . . ."

He was interrupted by a bang in the distance.

A tongue of flame shot into the air.

"Whatever was that?" said Mrs Fooby-Lartil.

Something silver and shiny zinged through the sky above the Town Hall.

"Well, Merry Christmas," said Mr Fooby-Lartil to Mrs Fooby-Lartil and Percy. "My

best present yet. My Troublefree-Teamaker's exploded again and blown a great big hole in the Mayor's roof."

"Serves him right," said Percy.

"Funny though," said Mr Fooby-Lartil. "I thought I'd cracked it this time."

Percy snorted. He turned the red leather steering wheel and pulled the power-assisted steering handle. The buggy swung round and the babies clapped and waved. "Home," said Percy. "We've got all the leftovers to finish before bed." He turned to the Fooby-Lartils. "You can catch us up," he said. "We'll go on ahead."

The Fooby-Lartils watched as he drove the buggy away.

"One way and the other," said Mr Fooby-Lartil, "we've had a very busy year."

"Full of unexpected things," said Mrs Fooby-Lartil, stroking the piglet's snout.

"Well," said Mr Fooby-Lartil cheerfully, "at least all our troubles are over now."

Mrs Fooby-Lartil stared at Percy and the babies vanishing into the distance. "I don't know," she said with a frown. "I have the strangest feeling they may be only just beginning."